Small Town Christmas

a Blue Harbor novel

OLIVIA MILES

Rosewood Press

ALSO BY OLIVIA MILES

Blue Harbor Series
A Place for Us
Second Chance Summer
Because of You

Stand-Alone Titles
Meet Me at Sunset
This Christmas

Oyster Bay Series
Feels Like Home
Along Came You
Maybe This Time
This Thing Called Love
Those Summer Nights
Christmas at the Cottage
Still the One
One Fine Day
Had to Be You

Misty Point Series
One Week to the Wedding
The Winter Wedding Plan

Sweeter in the City Series
Sweeter in the Summer
Sweeter Than Sunshine
No Sweeter Love
One Sweet Christmas

Briar Creek Series
Mistletoe on Main Street
A Match Made on Main Street
Hope Springs on Main Street
Love Blooms on Main Street
Christmas Comes to Main Street

Harlequin Special Edition
'Twas the Week Before Christmas
Recipe for Romance

ISBN: 978-1-7346208-4-9

Publisher's Note: This is a work of fiction. Names, characters, places, and incidents are a product of the author's imagination. Locales and public names are sometimes used for atmospheric purposes. Any resemblance to actual people, living or dead, or to businesses, companies, events, institutions, or locales is completely coincidental.

Small Town Christmas

1

Cora Conway popped open the box for her window display with the same sense of thrill that she experienced each year when it was time for the task. She knew that some people might think it was silly to put such effort into her annual Christmas window when she ran a year-round holiday shop, but it was tradition, and Cora loved nothing more than upholding traditions.

And that was why, every year, on Thanksgiving Day when the store was closed, she spent the better part of the afternoon putting out the personal decorations that would not be on sale come tomorrow, when the shoppers decided to come in by the dozens, stuffed with turkey and cranberry sauce and pumpkin pie, ready to think about their next holiday. She had many decorations that were passed down from her grandparents to her mother and then, because she loved them the most of the four sisters, to her.

There were the nutcrackers and the porcelain village pieces, and the angels with delicate, gilded wings. There were the snowmen, and the snowflakes that sparkled when they caught the winter light.

But first, there was mistletoe.

Cora pulled her ladder to the front of the store, careful not to bump one of the many display tables that were

overflowing with seasonal items, and stopped just beside the front door where she always hung a giant ball of mistletoe by a thick, velvet ribbon. She purchased it from the tree lot next door (yes, another tradition), because the only fake greenery she liked were the twelve-themed trees that filled the meandering rooms of her shop, and even then, she always kept a pine-scented candle lit to set the mood.

She climbed carefully, knowing from her father's recent experience that it wasn't always wise to climb a ladder when no one else was around unless you wanted to end up with a broken bone or two, but she had done this many times before, and besides, she was due at her childhood home for dinner in less than an hour. Surely, one of her sisters or cousins would come looking for her if she didn't show up—especially since she was in charge of the butternut squash casserole this year. She was no cook, and it was hardly her favorite side dish, but it was the only bargaining chip she had with her father's girlfriend, who loved nothing more than decorating a table. If Cora could only have one holiday to be in charge of overseeing, she called Christmas, leaving Candy with Thanksgiving, and Cora with…squash.

Of course, Candy had already thought of a wonderful idea for Christmas. Candy had hoped to create a candy cane theme, no surprise there. She'd been sure to let them know every chance she had, but Cora was planning on something more elegant. Something that went with the theme of this year's window display at her shop: White Christmas, just like the snow that was already started to fall outside, covering Blue Harbor's Main Street in a quiet blanket, and filling Cora with all the feels that she lived for, year-round. Here at Harbor Holidays, she was always surrounded by carols and the smell of cinnamon and cloves. Even on the hottest of summer days, when tourists flocked to the small, lakefront Michigan town, they came into her store and smiled.

Christmas made people happy. It brought out the best in them. And it brought out the best in this town.

And maybe, Cora thought, as she reached her arm as high as she could, feeling for the hook, with the help of this mistletoe, it would eventually bring her a little romance, too.

She finally felt the ribbon catch when there was a jostling of the ladder and the jingle bells over the door jangled, and Cora felt herself get precariously close to losing her step. She cried out, her arms reaching for the tree topper on her nearest themed tree (also White Christmas, just for this year) but instead, she felt a strong hand on her wrist.

She looked down to see warm gray eyes staring back at her with the slightest sheen of amusement when it was established that she was, indeed, okay.

Her heart began to beat quickly, and this time, it had nothing to do with nearly falling off a ladder. Dark hair. Strong jaw. Swoon-worthy grin.

"I didn't mean to startle you," the man apologized.

"We're not open today," she said, regretfully, knowing that she would gladly make the exception and not wanting him to make a quick departure, either.

"Of course." The man shook his head, looking doubtful for standing there, and set a hand on the doorknob. "It's Thanksgiving. I saw the light on, and I thought I would try."

Cora glanced at her box of decorations and then at the coo-coo clock on the wall (Nutcracker-themed, and not for sale!) and knew with regret that she couldn't invite him to stay even if she wanted to.

And oh, did she want to.

"I'm afraid I'm just wrapping up. No pun intended," she added with a smile, before immediately giving herself an internal kick. It wasn't every day that handsome men walked into her shop, not unless they were on the hand of a wife or girlfriend, and she was a little out of practice when it came to the art of flirtation. She stepped off the ladder, only realizing then that the man was tall, and age-appropriate, too. Early to mid-thirties, she'd say, with the faintest laugh lines at the corners of his eyes that made him feel approachable. From the expensive wool coat and slick leather shoes he was wearing, she pegged him for a tourist, city stock, no doubt. But then, it was a holiday. Perhaps he was just dressed up for the day.

Likely, he was just in town for the day.

Still, it wouldn't hurt to ask. "But we open early tomorrow?"

She framed it by way of invitation, hoping that he would see that she wanted him to return, and not just because she could use the sale.

"Of course. It's a holiday. You must have plans."

"Family dinner," she said, nodding. "I don't think my sisters would ever forgive me if I let the turkey go cold."

The man seemed to look panic-stricken for a moment, before rubbing a hand over his jaw. "Turkey, right. That's what people usually do on Thanksgiving, isn't it?"

Cora frowned at the man, wondering if this was some sort of joke or attempt at banter, but realized by the bewildered expression that had come over his face that he was dead serious. He scanned the room for a moment, as if he was trying to think, or remember something, and then took a step back, sighing with what seemed to be regret.

Cora bit back her own sigh of the exact same feelings. Turkey was great, and she usually loved Thanksgiving, but right now, standing alone in this shop with this man, she couldn't help but feel the urge to start some new traditions. Ones that would nicely start right under this ball of mistletoe.

"Tomorrow then," he said, nodding.

"I'll be here," she said, smiling broadly, and hoping she was simply coming across as friendly, rather than eager. "Happy Thanksgiving!" she added, showing her hospitality. After all, at Harbor Holidays, there was something for every season and holiday, even Halloween. A girl had to do what a girl had to do around here.

"Of course." The man looked distracted as he pulled open the door, letting a gust of icy wind float through the usually warm and cozy space. "Happy Thanksgiving."

He gave her a grin that made her knees go more than a little weak, and then disappeared out onto the quiet street, where the snow immediately began to gather on his dark hair. Cora pretended to straighten the sign on her door as she watched him go, wondering just exactly what that was all about and if she really would see him again.

She glanced up at the mistletoe that hung above the ladder and bit her lip to hide her smile, just in case he happened to be looking back.

Tomorrow. She didn't know how she'd sleep through the night, but luckily, a big turkey dinner with all the fixings might just do the trick.

*

Phil opened the door to his luxury SUV and slid onto the heated seat, even though the silent fumes coming from his daughter had kept him all too warm and uncomfortable for the entire drive from Chicago. He'd hoped to make the visit to the holiday shop quick, nothing more than an errand, really—and he had—but he hadn't accomplished what he'd set out to do. He'd been too distracted by the fumble at the door, the harried but tense road trip, and the pressure of everything he was missing back in the office taking not just today but tomorrow off as well.

And he'd been admittedly disarmed by the sweet smile of the shop girl, and the warmth of her blue eyes. And then there was the matter of Thanksgiving! He had the nagging feeling that take-out wasn't an option.

"Everything looks closed," Georgie finally said, sharing his sentiments. The stretch of downtown Blue Harbor was dark, well, other than the overwhelming amount of twinkling lights.

Honestly! Thanksgiving wasn't even over yet and they were already in full Christmas mode?

Wryly, he supposed the city was no different. He just hadn't taken the time to pay it much attention. Besides, in the city, he was busy. The days blurred together. Whereas in Blue Harbor…everything was different.

He swept his eyes up the street again and over to his daughter, daring to hope that he'd be able to turn that frown around with the promise of a better day tomorrow, because he was clear out of options for tonight. Even the inns looked dark.

Trying his best smile, Phil said, "Maybe there's food at the house."

"Why would there be food at the house?" For a nine-year-old, Georgie was very perceptive. She paid attention, and she remembered everything. Something he should keep in mind from now on, or at least until she went back to her mother's house.

"I thought you said that no one lives there," Georgie pointed out. "That Great-Grandma and Grandpa hadn't lived there for almost a year."

Damn. She was right. He'd stupidly hoped that the grocery store would be open, but the only storefront with the lights on in all of downtown came from the holiday shop. Of all places.

He eyed it now. The converted Victorian home at the edge of Main Street was crowded from the floor to the ceiling with tchotchkes and dust catchers. The woman who had worked there had been nice enough, though, meaning with any luck, she wouldn't cause trouble. She was pleasant. Pretty, too.

He thinned his lips. Well. No need to go down that path. He was in town for a reason. And that reason was currently overshadowed by the fact that it was Thanksgiving Day, he didn't have a turkey much less a slice of pie to offer his daughter, and against his wishful thinking, she wasn't willing to part with these traditions.

He was failing. Day one of getting a little time with his daughter and he was already mucking it up, just like his ex-wife had always insisted he would.

"I'll make you a big turkey dinner this weekend. Tomorrow, in fact," he promised, remembering that the woman in the holiday shop had told him she was open the next morning. Surely every other store would be too. And restaurants, too, he thought, knowing that he wasn't much of a cook, whereas Georgie's mother was one step away from being an official gourmet.

Not that he'd had much experience appreciating her culinary efforts. Even when they were married, most of his dinners were business-related: with clients, or in the office, surrounded by take-out containers.

"You know how to cook a turkey?"

Shoot. She was on to him again. "We can learn together. Can't be that hard, right?"

Georgie raised a single eyebrow. Her silence spoke her true thoughts on the matter, and he was fairly certain that they matched his own.

"It won't be the same if we do it tomorrow," Georgie eventually grumbled. "Just forget it. This is the worst Thanksgiving ever!"

"Well, now, I won't say it's the *worst* Thanksgiving ever," he chided, pulling up a memory of one particularly disastrous holiday, and the last he ever spent here in this town. It was Thanksgiving, he was in his senior year of college, already accepted to a competitive MBA program by early admission, and his father had reluctantly agreed to a weekend in his small, Michigan hometown after Phil's grandfather's recent stroke. He had recovered well—that time. Well enough to tell Phil's father exactly what he thought of him, and his priorities.

Phil had looked on, silenced, wondering if his father cared that they weren't proud, knowing how badly that must have hurt, even if his father didn't say anything in response.

They'd left that night. Before the timer had even popped on the turkey. They'd stopped at a pizza joint somewhere near the state border, his mother sipping her wine nervously, his father glaring at the table. That had been the last time that Phil had come to this town. It was also the last time that his father had ever spoken to his parents.

But that wasn't a story for a nine-year-old. And from the looks of it, Georgie wasn't interested in hearing it, either.

Right. Time for an executive decision. Usually, Phil ate his turkey and mashed potatoes in a hotel in the city, if he bothered with the silly tradition at all. Sometimes he didn't even remember it was Thanksgiving; work kept him too busy for those sorts of trivial interruptions. But it was late, the town was closed, and Georgie had made a point that they would not find any provisions at his grandparents' house.

He turned the car around and backtracked ten minutes to the gas station on the edge of town, where, inside he grabbed two frozen pizzas, some instant coffee, a gallon of milk, and a handful of whatever treats he thought might put a smile on his daughter's face. Yet again, Georgie preferred to sit in the warm car rather than accompany him on the errand. He wasn't going to argue with her, or push her. They weren't used to spending time together since the divorce, when her mother moved her out to California.

He pushed back the guilt that reared as he handed over a twenty-dollar bill and gathered up the bags. According to his ex, he hadn't spent enough time with his daughter long before that. He'd been too busy providing, or so the argument went. And that argument, well, that was just one more thing that hadn't changed since the divorce.

Back in the car, Georgie cranked up the volume on the radio when he tried to cajole her with a candy bar—her favorite kind, too.

Christmas music, he thought with annoyance. It was still November! But then, as he knew all too well, Blue Harbor loved the holidays…

He turned down the dial, slanting her a glance while he kept his focus on the road. "Look, Georgie, I'm sorry. I didn't plan ahead and I assumed that some restaurants would be open. Things are different in small towns."

Very different, he thought, as he wound his way down the dark streets toward town for the second time. It was already growing dark and he turned on his bright lights for better vision. The last thing he needed was to hit a deer or get into an accident on Thanksgiving evening in this remote area.

As a kid, he'd enjoyed a few summer weeks in Blue Harbor, splashing in the lake, and learning to fish from his grandfather. His parents saw it as a way to get him out of the city so he wasn't underfoot when school was out of session, and he didn't complain. Unlike in the city, here he could wake to the sunlight streaming through the window, to the sound of birds calling over the open water, and stay up late enough to see the stars fill the sky. His grandmother always cooked his favorite foods, and they would eat together outside on the faded picnic table, or inside, at the cramped kitchen table. It wasn't exciting, but it was peaceful, and very different from his life back in the city.

His real life, he had to remind himself.

Now he'd much prefer to be back in the comfort of his high-rise apartment, with fifty different take-out menus at the ready. But business was business and he was never one to be irresponsible when it came to that.

Parenting, on the other hand…He sucked in a breath. That was one thing he'd always tried to get right, but unlike every other relationship he had, he had the sinking feeling that he was coming up short.

Now was the chance to change that. He had to do better.

"Tell you what," he said, grinning at his daughter even though she didn't match his effort. "To make up for letting you down today, you can choose anything you want that will make up for it."

As he slid to a stop at the intersection, he saw her eyes widen with interest. "*Anything*?"

He smiled. "Well, it can't be too crazy. I can't buy you a llama or something. I can't fly you to the moon."

Couldn't turn back time either, he thought with a heavy heart he pushed away by tightening his grip on the steering wheel.

She giggled now, a sound that made him nearly sigh in relief. "So we're good? Even with pizza for Thanksgiving?"

"As long as it's plain cheese," she said, narrowing her eyes, but she couldn't fight the smile this time, and just for a moment, Phil dared to think that this trip might not be so bad after all.

*

So much for tradition. Cora stood inside the lakefront Victorian home where she and her sisters had spent many magical holidays, and stared in dismay at the dining room table, where a giant cardboard cut-out of a turkey was taking center stage where the real bird should be placed after being carved. Candy was trussed up in an apron with a giant turkey face on it, and in lieu of ruffles, there were fabric turkey feathers for the trim.

Cora caught her sister Amelia's eye across the room but quickly looked away. They had a way of sharing their deepest, innermost thoughts with the slightest widening of the eye, and all it took was one glance before the giggles caught on, and trying as Candy could be, the last thing Cora wanted to do was hurt the woman's feelings. She had clearly put a lot of thought into the day, even if she did seem to think she was hosting a group of school-age children, rather than four young women in their twenties and thirties. And besides, Cora was feeling generous.

"I bet Keira will love this," Cora offered. "What time are Britt and Robbie coming?"

Amelia answered, "The Bradfords eat earlier in the day, so they should be here soon. Britt said they were stopping by the orchard for another bottle of wine."

"Don't we have plenty here?" Their eldest sister now managed the family orchard and winery, and it wasn't like her to be anything less than punctual. But then, reuniting with her high school sweetheart and his adorable little girl had done wonders for her mood these days. As had coming back to town.

It was their first Thanksgiving all together in over a decade.

Well, *almost* all together, Cora thought, letting her eyes drift to the chair nearest the kitchen where their mother always sat.

She swallowed back that thought before her heart grew too heavy to enjoy the day, and said to Amelia, "Did Matt join them? You didn't want to go?"

Like Britt, Amelia had recently found love again, with Robbie's cousin. One by one, things were changing, and the table was growing. Cora couldn't help but wonder if this time next year she might have a reason to have an extra chair pulled up to the table.

Amelia shook her head. "I promised Candy I'd help cook for today." She gave Cora a knowing look. "Well, more like I promised Aunt Miriam."

Cora laughed. "I'm sure she's grateful."

Amelia was the best cook in town if anyone were to ask Cora, and she was certain that the devoted patrons of the Firefly Café would agree.

Candy on the other hand...Well, finger foods were more her specialty.

"Thanks for bringing the casserole. It was one less thing for me to do," Amelia added.

"I assume Maddie is bringing the pies?" She didn't need to ask, but with Candy, anything was possible.

"Apple and pumpkin!" Maddie cried out as she burst into the room, her cheeks rosy from the cold, her scarf wrapped tightly around her neck. Her boyfriend, Cole McCarthy, closed the door and locked it, before remembering where he was and unlocking it. The Conway residence was always open to any newcomer.

Even Candy, Cora reminded herself.

"The snow is really coming down out there," Cole observed, wiping his shoes on the mat.

Cora smiled at him. She knew that this holiday must be even more difficult for him than it was for her or her sisters. Sure, it was their first holiday with their father's girlfriend, but this was Cole's first holiday without his mother, who had passed away at the start of the month. She was happy to be able to welcome him into their home, to give him some distraction and companionship, however untraditional the night was shaping up to be. It was one of the things that she loved most about holidays, though Christmas in particular. It was the opportunity to welcome new faces or reunite with old ones, on a single night where bygones could be bygones, and everything was merry and happy and full of hope.

And hope she had, she thought with a little smile. Tomorrow morning that handsome stranger just might come into her store, and this time, she'd be ready.

As with all holidays in the Conway home, there was a flourish of activity as everyone arrived and they prepared the table, careful not to upset any of Candy's homemade decorations. Even cousin Gabby, who owned the flower shop in town, set her stunning red and orange arrangement on the buffet so it wouldn't upstage Candy's efforts. Chairs were pulled back, and room was made for others to slide in, and among all the happy chaos that reminded Cora why she loved being part of a big family, her father caught her eye across the room.

"I wanted to give you something," he said, motioning for her to follow him.

Cora glanced at the table, where Britt was helping Keira to a glass of sparkling cider, and Robbie and Matt were politely warning everyone that their stomachs were already full. Aunt Miriam was already scolding Uncle Steve to go easy on the butter and mind his cholesterol, and

Britt was asking cousin Jenna what time Miriam's sister and her family would arrive for dessert.

Seeing as Natalie Clark worked during the winter season for Cora when the ferries stopped running out to Evening Island where she usually worked at a big summer resort, Cora had it on good authority that the Clarks would be arriving at seven. It was their tradition to all come together, including Aunt Miriam's family along with the Conways, and Cora was already looking forward to the second part of the evening.

"Don't you need to carve the turkey?" Cora asked worriedly. It was tradition, after all, and she wasn't exactly sure what would happen to the poor bird if Candy took the task upon herself.

"This won't take a minute, and I didn't want to forget. You know how these nights can go."

She smiled at him as they stopped in his study. These nights were long. There would be food, and laughter, and wine, and then there would be dishes and dessert and more dishes, and then games and music, and more wine. Their family was in the business of wine, after all. And it was a holiday.

Dennis reached over and pulled a box from his desk. "I found this when I was up in the attic, rummaging through our old Christmas decorations. I don't think we've had this out for years, but once I saw it, I knew it was something you should have."

Of course. Everyone always wanted to give Cora their old Christmas decorations, even if some of it wasn't exactly worth keeping. But this, this was something from the attic of her childhood home. Meaning that maybe…

"It was your mother's," he said, reading her thoughts.

Cora looked up at him, seeing the mist in his eyes, even though the room was dim, only lit by a single lamp in the corner.

Carefully, she pulled back the tissue, revealing a snow globe with a charming village scene inside.

"I'm afraid it doesn't play music anymore," he warned.

"It doesn't have to," Cora said, feeling her own tears threaten to fall. "It's perfect just as it is."

"Your mother loved nothing more than a small-town Christmas," Dennis said. "This was one of her most prized possessions. I thought it was lost. Or broken. Your mother bought this the first Christmas we were married. She said that every time she looked at it, she remembered that wishes can come true."

"A Christmas wish always finds a way of coming true," Cora murmured. She looked at her father sharply. "She used to say that, too."

Dennis straightened his back. "She'd want you to have it. She'd be so proud of all the traditions you've kept going for our family. I am, too, even if I haven't said it enough."

"I know," Cora said as she carefully set the snow globe back in the box. Sensing that her father's mood was shifting, as she did with every holiday, she did her best to turn things onto more cheerful territory. "And that's why I think it's really important that we get back out there so you can carve that turkey."

Dennis laughed and pulled her in for a quick hug before planting a kiss on the top of her head.

From the dining room, they heard Amelia call out, "No touching those potatoes until the turkey is carved!"

"Some things never change," Dennis said, shaking his head.

Cora grinned up at him. "Some things aren't supposed to."

2

Cora stood behind the counter of her shop the next morning, wearing her "lucky" Black Friday sweater—the very same sweater she wore to kick off the official start to the holiday season each year. Granted, it was red, and the color wasn't exactly the most suitable for redheads, even if her hair was more auburn, like her father's. But it was soft against her skin and cozy enough to keep the chill away every time the door opened and the jingle bells jangled to alert her that a new customer had entered.

The bells had been ringing all morning, and while usually the sound faded into the background of the carols she had playing over the speakers, today Cora was on high alert. She darted her gaze to the paned door again, hoping to see the handsome man from yesterday, but it was just a little girl in a puffer coat.

Still, Cora couldn't help but smile at the way the child's eyes lit up and a gasp overtook her before her face broke out into a smile. She had dark curls that fell to her shoulders under her knitted hat, and the oversized pom-pom was comically toppled to the side.

Cora walked over to her, holding a plate of cut-out cookies that she'd commissioned Maddie to make special for today.

"Would you like a cookie?" she asked, and then, thinking the better of it, added, "Or do you need to ask your parents first?"

"I'm nine years old. I know the rules." The little girl licked her bottom lip in anticipation as she hovered her hand over the plate, clearly torn between the sparkly sugar cookie in the shape of a mitten and the equally sparkly cookie in the shape of a wreath.

She went for the mitten, the larger of the two.

"We have hot cocoa at the back of the store, too," Cora said. It was a hazard, she knew, to be offering beverages in her store, especially when everyone was crammed together in their bulky winter outerwear, but luckily, despite the amount of products she had on display, most people were very careful. Sure, things did break from time to time, but over the years she'd learned to place the more valuable items at higher reach, both on the shelves and on the trees.

"Oh, goody!" the little girl said through a bite of cookie. "You know, this cookie is way better than the ones I had for dessert last night."

Cora looked at her with interest. "You didn't have pie on Thanksgiving?"

The little girl frowned briefly. "No. My dad forgot. But that's okay," she said, with a shrug. "He said that I could pick anything I wanted to make up for it."

"Anything?" Cora bit her lip to keep from laughing. She supposed that failing to give this sweet little girl a proper Thanksgiving dinner was worth a big favor.

"Well, anything he can buy, like a toy or doll. I can't ask for a dog or anything." Now the little girl frowned again, deeper this time, and Cora felt so bad that she held out the cookie tray and gave the girl a wink. Immediately, the little girl lit up like Cora's brightest Christmas tree.

"A dog is a very big responsibility," Cora said, not that she would know. She herself would love a furry companion, but with her work at the store, she knew that she wouldn't be home long enough to give it the exercise and attention it deserved, even if she did live just upstairs from the shop. She'd considered the possibility of allowing a dog to stay with her in the store all day (she'd name it something festive like Merry or Dasher), but again…there were just so many products. It wouldn't have space to roam.

"My mom said that it wouldn't be fair to take a dog back and forth between two houses, especially all the way to California," the child said sagely. "And my dad doesn't even have a house. He has an apartment. No yard or anything."

"I see," Cora said, hiding a smile.

"But my mom and Arthur are moving to Indiana soon and that will be closer to my dad, so maybe I'll ask again." The little girl looked troubled. "But I think that my stepdad might be allergic."

Now Cora frowned. "Tell you what," she said, determined to cheer up the child and also noticing that a line had begun to form at the counter. She noticed Gladys O'Leary, who seemed to be making a dramatic gesture of sighing and tapping her foot, even though it was plain as day that Cora was standing just a few feet away. "You go help yourself to some hot chocolate and look around the store, and when you're ready, I'll show you my Christmas wishing ball."

"A Christmas wishing ball?" The little girl's gray eyes were round and bright, in sharp contrast with her dark hair.

"Well, it's a snow globe, really, but a very special one," Cora explained. She'd taken great pride in setting the new addition to her shop on the counter this morning, almost daring to feel her mother's presence was with her. "Sometimes the best things we can ask for can't be bought."

Now she glanced back at the counter again, suppressing one of her own sighs as Gladys gave her an obvious glare. A former shop owner herself, Gladys was likely to give Cora some unsolicited advice on customer service. Of course, of all times, Cora's seasonal assistant was on break.

"Be sure to check out all the rooms," she told the child. "In fact, I have one room of all pink ornaments."

"Pink for Christmas?" The little girl giggled.

Cora shrugged. "Did you ever see *The Nutcracker*?" She received an affirmative nod of the head. "It's the land of the sweets!"

Now the little girl scampered off without another word, and Cora was left to tend to Gladys, who made sure to pinch her lips long and hard enough for Cora to finally acknowledge her wait.

"Ah, a beautiful choice this year!" she said instead, refusing to have anyone muddle with her holiday spirit, even if she was starting to get in her own way of it.

She eyed the door again as the bell jangled. Nope. It was just one of her old schoolmates and her husband, not that she wasn't happy to see them.

Gladys cleared her throat again, and Cora snapped back to her duties. Each year, Gladys added to her Christmas village, and this year's piece was one of Cora's personal favorites: a skating rink surrounded by snow-frocked trees.

She wrapped it carefully, secured the box with the red bow that was signature to the shop, and handed over the equally red bag. "Have a merry day!" she said, as she did on occasion. Today, it felt a little forced.

She helped a few more people, all of whom she knew, of course. That was life in Blue Harbor for you. The small, lakefront Michigan town was far north and didn't see many tourists this time of year. Her mind wandered back to the man from yesterday. He was probably passing through, in town for the holiday, probably in need of a last-minute gift for the hostess. No sense in pinning her hopes to anything there. Really, she should know better.

She should. Except when she finally finished ringing up the last person in line and then scooted to the front display table to straighten some of the miniature trees, her breath caught when she saw the door swing open and the very man from yesterday appear.

Her heart was beating faster than the drum in the carol playing over the speaker, and she swallowed hard, hoping she didn't look quite as pleased as she felt, as she grinned.

"Welcome back!" she said warmly. *Play it cool, Cora.* But her cheeks were warm, and thanks to her fair complexion, she knew that they were probably bright pink, too. No poker face for her.

"You remember me," he observed, seeming amused by this.

Yep, city stock. As if that wasn't obvious by his attire, yet again. Meaning that he would probably be gone by Sunday. She stifled a sigh as the disappointment landed squarely in her chest.

"Small-town life," she said with a shrug. "Everyone knows everyone."

"Then you have me at a disadvantage," he said, removing an expensive-looking leather glove and extending his hand.

"Cora Conway," she said, slipping her hand in it. Oh, it was warm and smooth and large enough to cover her own. She could have lingered there half the day, but instead, she did the professional thing and pulled it away, her gaze still holding his.

A little furrow formed between his brow, and he studied her for a moment. "Do you own this shop?"

"I sure do," she said proudly. "And now I'm afraid you have me at a disadvantage."

He laughed, a low, deep sound that she liked. A lot.

"I'm—" He hesitated. "Phil."

"Phil…" She waited for his full name, but at that moment, the little girl from earlier burst to the front of the room, another cookie in her hand, and a cup of hot chocolate, too. One that looked like it could spill at any minute, and hopefully not on one of the white lace tablecloths or velvet Santas.

"Daddy! They have hot chocolate! And cookies! And there's an entire room of pink ornaments! And it all sparkles," she added, wistfully.

Phil laughed, and Cora could only look on with interest. This was the child's father? She tried to remember what the little girl had said. About Thanksgiving. About the dog. About her family situation.

She glanced back at Phil, who was taking in his daughter's excited chatter with a look of bewilderment and confusion.

"Watch the hot cocoa, Georgie," he urged. "You don't want to mess up anything in this pretty store."

"Oh, I'll be careful. I already found something I want, too."

Phil glanced at Cora with a bemused grin and let his daughter lead him to the back of the store. Cora watched with a quickening of her heart. She couldn't help it. Tourists came through Blue Harbor all the time. Summer season here was like a Midwest playground. No one had ever caught her attention like this before.

Before she had time to turn her thoughts back to reality, Georgie was back, holding a stuffed toy in the shape of a reindeer.

"We'll take the toy," Phil said.

"Of course!" Cora stepped behind the counter, wishing that their visit to the shop wasn't ending so quickly.

She took her time wrapping up the package. Georgie had swiped another cookie, not that she minded. She decided to use the opportunity to feel out the situation.

"Is this your first time in Blue Harbor?" she asked.

"I used to visit as a kid," Phil said distractedly. He pulled his wallet from his pocket and retrieved a credit card before changing his mind and pulling out some cash instead.

"Daddy lives in Chicago," Georgie informed her.

Cora hated the way her heart sank. Blue Harbor saw many tourists from Chicago. Her own sister Britt had lived there for years. It was just that Chicago was about half a day's drive away. And this man, well, he was just a Christmas fantasy, wasn't he?

She forced a smile. "Well, if you have a chance, you might want to stop by Buttercream Bakery. My younger sister owns it and she made those delicious cookies you like so much, Georgie. And I happen to know that right now, her store is full of Christmas treats."

"Can we, Daddy?" Georgie asked excitedly.

"I'm not sure we'll have time while we're in town, honey," Phil said, much to Cora's regret as much as Georgie's.

Georgie frowned dramatically and then shifted her stare to the snow globe on the counter. "Is this the wishing ball?" she asked Cora.

Cora was happy to prolong their visit. She leaned into the counter and waggled her eyebrows, playing along. "It is. Now, it doesn't play music anymore, but I think that's because it's more interested in listening than telling us something."

Georgie studied the snowy scene in the globe. "It looks like Blue Harbor."

Cora smiled, knowing this was why her mother loved it. "It does."

Georgie stood up straight and gave her father a stern look, one that said she meant business. "I know what I want, Daddy. To make up for pizza on Thanksgiving," she clarified.

Pizza on Thanksgiving? Cora raised an eyebrow and Phil winced. Adorable. And clearly guilty.

"I thought this toy was your make-up treat," he said, motioning the object that Cora was slowly wrapping.

Georgie shook her head. "This toy is because I can't have a dog, because you and Mommy live in separate houses and because Mommy's new husband is allergic."

Now it was Phil's turn to look pink in the cheeks. He flashed Cora a look of apology, but she just smiled and continued her wrapping. Slowly. So slowly.

"Okay, then, what'll it be? A trip to the bakery?" Phil's smile looked a little pained.

Georgie picked up the snow globe and said, "I want to spend my Christmas break here, in this town in the snow globe. In Blue Harbor."

Phil let out a tense laugh and scraped a hand through his hair. "Honey, remember what I said about asking for something within reason? I have business waiting for me in the city."

"You're always working!" Georgie cried. "Even at Christmas!"

"Christmas is just one day of the year, Georgie." Phil seemed to stiffen.

It took all of Cora's might not to comment on that. Christmas was an entire season. She should know. She'd made a business of it.

"You said you have business here," Georgie pointed out. "And you said that you would make up Thanksgiving to me. And this is our first Christmas together in a long time! And I don't have any school or anything because of the move!"

Phil blinked at his daughter while Cora held her breath at the exchange and pretended to be more interested in the toy she was wrapping.

"And besides, this is a Christmas wishing ball," Georgie said, smiling triumphantly. "And the nice lady said that whatever you wish for with this has to come true."

Phil flashed a look on Cora. Cora winced and held up her hands. Obviously, her vote was with Georgie, and her motive was only partly ulterior.

Phil shifted his gaze down to his daughter, a long, hard look that made Cora almost believe he was contemplating it, or thinking of how he could politely untangle himself from this situation without making a scene.

"I'll think about it," he finally said.

Georgie set the ball back on the counter and collected her parcel. "That means yes," she whispered.

Cora managed to keep her facial expression innocent as she collected the money and handed back the change.

"Come again while you're in town!" she said, holding Phil's gaze.

"Oh, you can bet on it," he said under his breath, giving her a rueful smile that told her that Georgie might just be right.

Still, just in case, Cora picked up the ball, closed her eyes, and made her own Christmas wish. Maybe there was a little Christmas magic in it, after all.

*

Phil decided that the bakery was as good as any place to park himself and Georgie for a while so he could look over the paperwork he'd gathered for his grandparents' properties. And it earned a few points in the parenting department, too. Right now, he needed all the credit he could get, but staying in Blue Harbor for nearly four weeks was not exactly a great idea.

Although, it wasn't necessarily a bad one either. The cottage needed work, or at least someone to arrange it if it was going to sell for what it was worth. A year of neglect had taken its toll; he should have come back sooner, dealt with this last summer, but work kept him from it, and now there was no more room for delay.

The Buttercream Bakery was just as enchanting as the holiday shop, and nearly as decorated, too. The front door greeted them with a wreath and a jingle, and the counter was lined with a long pine swag. The room was filled with Christmas music, and the smells that one could only associate with the season; even if traditional holidays were not something he had much personal experience with, the sweet spices immediately conjured up images of sitting around a crackling fireplace, or the base of a tree.

The bakery did not have a tree. There was no room, he quickly assessed, sweeping his gaze over the vibrant establishment which was clearly a popular destination in town. A young woman who was just as pretty as Cora stood behind the counter wearing a red apron and chatting happily to a customer at the head of the line. Georgie already had her nose to the glass of the display case while Phil looked up at the chalkboard menu on the wall, wondering if there was a single item that didn't contain the word "yuletide," "Christmas," or "Noel." There was no escaping the endless cheer. Not unless he went back to the city.

He finally decided on a plain black coffee. Georgie, on the other hand, announced to the woman behind the counter that she would like the candy cane cheesecake.

"You here for the long holiday weekend?" the woman who must clearly be the sister that Cora had mentioned asked with a pleasant smile. Perhaps sensing Phil's questioning glance, she added, "We get some new faces around here this time of the year. People visiting family…"

"No family. Not anymore, at least," Phil added. His grandparents hadn't lived in Blue Harbor since last winter, not since another stroke had made it too difficult for his grandfather to get by without around-the-clock care; something that was too much for his grandmother to take on. Now they lived in an assisted-living community in the Chicago suburbs. State of the art. He'd seen to it himself. Their only ties to this town were in the physical sense: the lakefront cottage, and the bigger Victorian on Main Street.

The holiday store, to be exact.

Cora was the owner of the holiday shop. He should have known it. It wasn't like these small businesses were teeming with staff. She was there on Thanksgiving Day. That should have been his first clue.

He supposed he should just be thankful that she didn't know who he was. Yet.

Phil was saved from having to further explain when a boisterous woman with bouncy blond curls and a necklace made of Christmas lights that flashed on and off, along with the matching earrings, burst in through a side doorway and said, "Maddie! Amelia's run out of flour next door and was wondering if we can borrow a pound or two?"

Phil glanced at the sign over the open doorway—Firefly Café—and back to the woman, who was giving him the once-over, and not so subtly. Both of their attention was pulled by a loud clearing of someone's throat.

Maddie gave Phil a look of apology and handed him his change, which he promptly dropped into the tip jar. From the looks of Georgie's treat, towered high with whipped cream and crushed candy canes, he suddenly wished he had indulged himself, but then, he was not in Blue Harbor for fun or festive cheer.

He was here on a mission. One which was probably going to be a little less clear-cut than he had first hoped.

"Go ahead and help yourself, Candy," the woman—Maddie—said. "My sister Amelia runs the café," she explained to him as the blond-haired woman disappeared through a side door. "Candy…well…she helps."

The hesitancy in her tone made Phil smile. "I'll have to check it out."

Maddie brightened. "Oh, it's a great place for dinner or lunch! Even won a state contest for one of the recipes!"

Phil took note of this. The kitchen situation at his grandparents' house was vintage at best, and Georgie would only eat so much frozen pizza. "Thanks, we might check it out later."

He settled into a table near the window, with a view of Lake Huron and beyond it, Evening Island. He smiled, his mind traveling back to another place and time, when he used to splash in the very water that was now cold and still or watch ferries cross to the island on long, summer days.

"I used to fish out there," he told his daughter now, musing over those carefree days.

"In a boat and everything?" Georgie shoveled a large piece of cheesecake into her mouth.

Phil nodded. He hadn't thought of that little motor boat in a long time. It wasn't much, and couldn't handle the days where the waves crashed against the shoreline, but it was small and manageable, and fun, he thought with sudden nostalgia.

He wondered what had ever happened to that boat. He regretted now that he'd never brought Georgie up here one summer to try it out.

Or Michelle. Maybe if he had, things would have turned out differently. Maybe she wouldn't have married Arthur, the accountant. Maybe she wouldn't have moved his daughter halfway across the country.

His gut tightened when he thought of their current circumstances. It was easy to blame his ex, but soon, she'd be moving Georgie back to the Midwest, because Art had a new job in Indiana. Then the only person he'd have to blame for his strained relationship with his daughter was himself.

"How's your reindeer?" he asked, motioning to the stuffed toy that was still hooked in the crook of Georgie's arm.

"He likes this bakery," she told him. She eagerly took another bite of her cupcake. "He likes this town. He thinks it would be much better to stay here than to go back to your apartment."

Phil frowned. "What's wrong with my apartment?" After the divorce, he'd downsized into a two-bedroom condo in one of Chicago's busier neighborhoods, where he could walk to his office and grab dinner from one of a hundred restaurants on the way home.

"You know, Daddy! It's sort of…sad." Georgie looked unfazed at this assessment as she continued to happily eat her treat.

Sad? Phil ran a hand over his chin. He supposed Georgie was right. He hadn't gotten around to decorating it much. Didn't see much reason to, really. But now, he realized that while functional, it might not be very inviting. Gray walls. A gray sofa. He never did get around to hanging artwork.

"Tell you what," he said, grinning. "When we get back, you can help me pick out a tree."

This was the first time since he and Michelle had split that he had four full weeks with Georgie, and that was only because Georgie's private school was closed for the term, and Georgie would be starting her new school in Indiana in January. Because Michelle was busy packing the house and needed him to help out "for once."

And because come January, Phil would be overseas, heading up their new European office. This time over the holidays would make up for all the time he'd be missing.

He let out a slow breath. Told himself for the hundredth time that it was what it was. That despite what Michelle said that he'd been a good father. Paid for the best schools, bought the best gifts, took her to the best restaurants.

But it sat as hollow as the feeling that he'd been a good son. That he'd been top of his class, been accepted to the best colleges, and ran a successful private equity firm. And that somehow, it still wasn't enough.

Georgie was shaking her head now. "I don't want to celebrate Christmas in Chicago. I want to stay here."

"What about the museums we were going to visit?" he asked. Technically, his assistant usually took her to the museums because work pulled him away, but he didn't see the point in highlighting that just now.

"I'm bored of museums," she reminded him, giving a dramatic pout.

He couldn't argue with her there. They'd bored him as a kid too, but his parents had still dragged him along—well, with the nanny. Now, he understood why they had done it. Education was important to him. Always had been. It was what set him up in life, for a good job, for a steady income, for success.

Where had it all gotten him, he wondered now, looking at his daughter, thinking of what Michelle had told him the day she'd ended their marriage. All he cared about was work, she'd said. And it had cost him his family.

Only this year, maybe it didn't have to. His staff was back at the office; they'd be working right up to the holiday, of course. He had his computer, his cell, and he could set up a home office from the dining room that obviously saw no other real use. It would be good training for the months and years ahead when he'd be setting up their European office, communicating remotely with the main branch in Chicago. But he wasn't in the mindset of taking time off work—not even for Christmas.

And that was something that his ex had never let him forget.

"Okay, if your mom agrees with it, we can stay here. But only until Christmas Day," he warned, barely believing the words that were coming out of his mouth. Good grief, was he really going to do this? Normally he'd be back at work the day after Thanksgiving. If he was being honest with himself, he was usually at the office on Thanksgiving.

His hands felt clammy when he considered his decision. Four weeks was a long time away from the office, with the days he had already missed. But four weeks as a single parent was an even bigger challenge. It might be easier here in Blue Harbor, really. His other game plan was to bring Georgie into the office most days, teach her about business, maybe have his assistant take her skating or shopping, or to look at the store windows on Michigan Avenue. At least here she could play outside, build a snowman. Do all the simple things that could only be found in this town.

Georgie whooped in excitement and stood up to fling her arms around his neck. "Oh, thank you, Daddy. This is going to be the best Christmas ever."

The best Christmas ever, huh? He certainly didn't know how to fulfill such a giant expectation, but he'd committed, and for now, at least, Georgie was happy. He knew that Michelle wouldn't protest—if anything, she'd be surprised that he was willing to take the time away from the office. He could hear it now, and his lip curled at the imaginary conversation. But he had the time off—even if he rarely took a day in the past, not even for Georgie's Kindergarten graduation, which had been the breaking point in their marriage.

And if he wanted to get his grandparents' properties cleaned up and ready for an easy sale, he'd have to put in some time and effort.

And something told him that despite her friendly disposition, Cora over at the Christmas shop wasn't going to make this easy for him in the slightest.

3

It was a tradition in the Conway family growing up that the day after Thanksgiving, they would trek into town to pick out a tree fresh from the lot—usually accompanied by an argument over which one was best.

Now that they were older, and each running their own businesses, that tradition had to be pushed off to Sunday afternoon, since Amelia closed Firefly Café early each Sunday and Maddie had followed suit when she opened the bakery.

Harbor Holidays was still open on Sunday—this was her biggest sales weekend of the year, after all—and Cora checked the clock now to see that she was finally going to be able to turn the sign on the door in ten minutes. Even with Natalie's help, she hadn't sat down all day or stopped for lunch, and the promise of warm hot chocolate, buttery cookies, and leftover turkey and cranberry sandwiches on toasted herb bread made her stomach rumble.

Loudly.

She laughed as a customer gave her a curious glance, and then added another ornament to their basket. It was one of Cora's favorites, and new this season. A frosted icicle that was part of her "White Christmas" tree, where everything was snowy and sparkly.

And magical.

Speaking of, she looked at the snow globe on the counter as she came back around to the main room to help ring up the last of the customers. Would her Christmas wish be coming true this year? She hadn't seen Phil or his daughter yesterday or today, but then she supposed that there wouldn't really be much reason for them to come back to the store, would there?

Besides, if they were staying in town, she would eventually run into them. There were only so many places to go, especially in the wintertime when the ferry stopped running out to Evening Island and the lakefront lost its usual traffic.

Cora finished with the remaining customers, sent Natalie home to spend time with her daughter, and then locked up with a tired sigh. She flicked off the lights, leaving only the strands of Christmas lights on, which, considering how many trees and how many lights she had, still made the store feel quite bright.

She paused in the kitchen at the back of the building only long enough to steal one remaining cut-out cookie she had tucked away for herself, and then dashed up the back stairs to her living quarters to get her warmest coat, hat, and gloves. She knew that most people would think she was crazy, walking all the way to her father's house when she had a perfectly functioning car. But she'd been cooped up all day, and she loved the smell of the air in the winter. The bite of the snow. The freshness of pine.

And she loved seeing their small, lakeside community veiled by the blanket of glistening snowfall.

With her scarf pulled tight, she let herself out the back door and came around to Main Street. The tree lot was conveniently located just beside her store, a happy coincidence that she had certainly taken into consideration when she'd first opened her store, even if she didn't really have any other options. Main Street was small, but packed with small businesses, and those shop owners who retired liked to pass their legacy down to grandkids, or sometimes, in the case of Cora, to those who would carry things on out of good old-fashioned nostalgia.

The house that Cora had rented out was actually once a primary residence for a sweet couple who moved out to a smaller cottage on the lake. Over the years they rented out the house on Main Street, even considered turning it into a small inn at one point, or so rumor had it. But Cora knew that it was meant to be a holiday shop just as much as she knew that she was meant to run it. And when the lease became available five years ago, she'd jumped at the chance.

"Hey there, Bart!" she called out to the man in the wooly jacket and sensible hat. His gloves were even no-nonsense, fit for a northern Michigan winter and long days spent grabbing trees by the trunk and securing them with twine to car roofs.

He gave her a wave. "Good weekend?"

She knew what he meant by that. He meant good sales. They'd had plenty of chats over the years about how difficult it could be to survive in such a seasonally driven business.

"It's the start of Christmas! It couldn't be better!" She paused long enough to feel the wind slice through her coat. "I hope my sisters picked a good one this year."

"I think it was Candy that did the picking," Bart replied with a knowing grin.

Cora felt her eyes hood. So there it was. Another change. Another break in tradition.

She could only hope that her sisters guided Candy in the right direction. Still, she braced herself for what might be standing in the big bay window of her childhood Victorian home. She supposed she should just be happy that, seeing as it was a fresh tree, it wouldn't be pink.

Not that she had a problem with pink trees. She had one in her store, after all.

Still, she felt her spirits slag a bit, and she raised her hand halfheartedly in goodbye when someone else raised their hand in hello.

She froze, the coldness no longer bothering her, or the wind either. It was Phil. And his daughter. Standing in the tree lot.

Did that mean that they were here to stay for the next few weeks?

"Hello," she said, smiling slowly as she crossed a few feet into the lot. Bart was busy helping old Mrs. Benson now, and given how picky she had been just a short hour ago in the store, Cora was fairly certain her indecisiveness would distract Bart long enough to keep him from picking up on Cora's obvious delight at seeing Phil.

Bart had been after her for years to find a little romance, after all, but then, he was yet to find any himself. More than once they'd lamented the fact they were just friends—which they were—because that's what happened when you knew someone as long as she and Bart had known each other. Since preschool to be exact. He was a sweet guy, and he was in the business of Christmas, but there wasn't a spark.

There wasn't…magic.

Whereas with Phil…

She let her gaze drift from Phil to Georgie, who was staring at the trees with obvious joy. She could see the resemblance more clearly now. The dark hair, the bright eyes. There was something else familiar about the little girl, though. Something she couldn't quite pinpoint.

"Is it safe to assume that your Christmas wish has come true?" She winked at the little girl and then smiled up at Phil, who looked less amused than she was.

"I have a very convincing daughter," he said wryly. "But it seems that you can't have a small-town Christmas without a tree, so…"

"You can't have any Christmas without a tree!" Cora said, laughing. "But then, I do own a holiday shop."

He gave her a funny look, and she wondered for a moment if her enthusiasm for the holiday was bordering on "too much" as her sisters sometimes accused her of over the years.

She paused, thinking of how, despite their complaints, they were always grateful for everything that she did, and always eagerly looked forward to the little traditions she kept alive, like tonight's tree decorating, for example.

Phil gestured to the tree he was holding by the trunk. "What do you think of this one?"

Cora hadn't even considered where they might be staying, but now her interest was piqued.

"It's beautiful, but it might be a bit large for one of the inns."

"Oh, we're staying in a house," Phil said tightly.

Cora didn't press. There were plenty of people in town who rented out vacation properties, though less so at this time of year. Still, if Phil had decided to go so far as to rent a house, that meant that he was committed to staying.

She couldn't hide her smile.

"I think it's perfect," Georgie said.

"I couldn't agree more." Cora shivered against a gust of wind. Maybe it was the shop owner in her, or maybe it was the thrill of a potential romance, but she added, "If you need some decorations for the tree, you know where to come."

"Right next door!" Georgie exclaimed. Then, after a brief pause, she asked, "Will you have cookies again?"

Cora laughed. "Every day of the holiday season," she promised. Maddie's bakery was new; it was her way of supporting her youngest sister, and so far the customers were all too happy with the addition.

"Then we'll be there!" Georgie said.

Cora gave Phil one last glance before she walked away. "I look forward to it."

*

Phil groaned under his breath. Georgie certainly wasn't making any of this easier for him, not that he could tell her that. She was a child, and she wanted a magical Christmas, and he could already tell that Blue Harbor was going to offer her more than his "sad" apartment back in Chicago ever could.

If that wasn't history repeating itself, he wasn't sure what was.

But it wasn't just the part about staying in town that was the issue. It was Cora, and her friendly way with Georgie. After all, what child wouldn't love a store like that at Christmastime? There were toys and lights and…a pink tree!

He smiled in spite of himself. He knew the answer to that question, and it was him. Growing up, Christmas was just another day of the year. His father saw it as his busy season—close to the year-end crunch. His mother saw it as a social season, a time for parties and toasts. There wasn't time to bother with a tree most years, and eventually, Phil stopped seeing the reason for one and started thinking practically, like his parents. Take this one, for example. He gripped the trunk and gave the branches a good hard shake. The needles would probably be long gone by Christmas. And then he'd have a mighty disappointed child on his hands. And that was the very last thing he wanted.

"Maybe we should get a fake tree," he said, thinking of all those trees in the holiday shop.

"No!" Georgie cried out. "You have to get a real tree! And this one is perfect!" She attempted to give the tree a hug, but knowing that would most certainly add to his concern about the needles falling off, he pulled it to the side.

"Fine," he sighed. A fake tree would be just one more item to get rid of when he cleared out his grandparents' cottage. "A real tree it is. But that's it. I've fulfilled my promise. You wanted to stay in Blue Harbor through Christmas, and now we are. Complete with a tree."

Georgie shook her head. "You can't have a tree without ornaments, Daddy."

"I'll get you some materials to make some then," he said, jutting his chin to the man in the trailer that was edged with twinkling lights. He glanced down at his daughter. "It will keep you busy while I work tomorrow."

"Work!" Georgie crossed her arms and pouted dramatically.

"Yes, while I work. My work doesn't stop just because it's Christmas. I have meetings and calls. And I have to work on the house." And at some point he needed to get over to the Christmas tree shop—but not for the reasons that Georgie had in mind.

A notice of lease termination needed to be delivered. Something he should have done on Thanksgiving Day, as intended.

The man with the name tag of Bart took his card and rang it through. "Need help tying it to your hood?"

Phil glanced at his daughter, swearing he saw a challenge in her eyes. "I'm good," he said tightly.

He resisted the urge to swear under his breath. He'd never tied a tree to a hood before, but really, how hard could it be?

Ten minutes later, sweating so much that despite the temperature, he'd had to loosen his scarf and had the urge to shed his coat, he could feel the heat of his daughter's eyes on his back as he wrestled the massive tree onto the hood, wondering just what kind of damage it was doing to his paint finish.

"You sure you don't need a hand?" Bart called out, and Phil could hear the trace of amusement in his voice.

He flashed a look at his daughter. "You wanted this, so you can help."

"Only if you say we can decorate it. For real," she added, for good measure.

She'd make a fine attorney one day, Phil thought ruefully. Just like his father. Still, he was desperate. And he suspected that she knew it.

"Fine. Now, open the door on the other side and climb in. Grab this rope when I pass it to you, okay?"

She nodded and did as she was told. Another ten minutes later, and not without more than one slipped curse word that his daughter reprimanded him for, the tree was secured to the roof of the car.

Sort of.

"We did it." Phil didn't know why he felt so triumphant, but he did, and it might have been partly because of the joy in his daughter's eyes as she looked up and admired their effort.

"We make a pretty good team, don't we?" Phil said, putting his arm around her.

She beamed up at him: a look he hadn't seen in a long time. If ever.

"The best, Daddy."

*

Cora stared at the tree that had been set up in the front room's bay window with a critical eye. After heavy scrutiny, she determined that she couldn't really find fault with it—something she knew should technically delight—not disappoint—her. The proportions were even, the color was an attractive shade of deep forest green, the needles were thick and healthy, and the branches were evenly distributed for the boxes of ornaments that her father was carrying down from the attic.

Britt, of course, was the first to say, "Are you being careful, Dad? I can call Robbie over here to help, you know."

He brushed away her concern with a deep and lingering frown. Ever since he'd broken his leg and arm last spring, Britt's fussing had been merciless, even worse than Amelia's, who had always been the most nurturing of the four sisters, and clearly, it was no longer appreciated.

Cora was secretly pleased that they'd decided not to include significant others tonight, even if she did wonder if it was because she was currently the only unattached sister. But having them together, with their childhood ornaments, the carols playing over the speaker, and the fire crackling in the hearth, was a tradition that was special to them, and she liked that it wasn't yet diluted by having to share it with anyone else.

Anyone other than Candy, that was, she thought, as Candy followed their father down the stairs, holding a box that most definitely didn't match the others.

Technically, Candy still had a condo in the neighboring town of Pine Falls, but from what Cora and her sisters could gather, she had all but moved into the Conway family home, or at least, she was hell-bent on putting her personal mark on it.

"Now, I know that you all usually put an angel on the top of the tree," Candy began, and immediately Cora felt her heart race with panic.

She glanced at her father, who shifted his gaze, and then to Amelia, who was not only the mother hen of the group but also the most diplomatic of the sisters. Amelia looked just as concerned as Cora felt, and seemed to open her mouth and then close it as if she wasn't even quite sure what to say.

"But I couldn't wait to share my star tree topper with you all," Candy continued as she unwrapped a giant, gold and red object with a flourish.

The room fell silent. Cora felt the blood rushing in her ears. It wasn't that there was anything wrong with the tree topper; in fairness, she sold something similar in the shop. But this was her family home. This was their tree. Their tradition. And the angel was part of it.

She glanced at her sisters, wondering who would speak up first, and then decided that since she had been the self-appointed keeper of the holidays since their mother's passing, the responsibility fell squarely on her shoulders.

"That's a lovely star, Candy, but we've always had the angel on our tree. We used to take turns growing up, each year one of us had the chance to finish off the decorating with it. It's...well, it's tradition."

Really, did anything more need to be said? Tradition was not something that you argued with, not in Cora's world. Not in the Conway house. And definitely not at Christmastime!

"Oh, I know, honey, and it's such a lovely angel. I just thought that, well, when Denny here offered to let me be included, that I might introduce something personal to my holiday. A new tradition, if you will."

Cora was aware that every eye in the room was on her, waiting for approval. Technically the angel was just wood and paint and fabric. But it held years of memories that had meant the world to her. Granted, they never argued over whose turn it was to put the thing up anymore. By the time they hit their teen years, they'd all just happily handed the task to Cora, but it was still a task that was performed, without fail. Was it ridiculous at her age that she needed to see that angel on the top of this tree?

"And all the ornaments are still your traditions," Candy pressed. "And look! We can put the angel right here, on the mantle. Won't that look sweet?" She plucked the object from the coffee table and walked over to the fireplace, smiling hopefully.

Cora glanced at her sister Britt, who gave her a little shrug as to say that it didn't bother her if the angel sat in the middle of the mantle, where it was at risk of getting roused and toppling over and falling into the flames below. Sure, that was probably unlikely, but not completely out of the question.

She gave a pleading look to Maddie. As the youngest, Maddie had often jockeyed for a chance to put up that angel, after all, and her eyes would shine in awe once it was up. But Maddie just gave her a little wince. It was only then that Cora remembered, of course, that Candy had set up Maddie and Cole. An unlikely pairing that couldn't have been a more perfect match than marshmallows and hot cocoa. Maddie was indebted now.

Sensing that she was outnumbered, Cora swallowed hard and said, "Whatever you all want."

"Thank you, Cora," her father whispered to her, as he popped the lid on another box.

Cora felt her heart sink as she set down her hot chocolate and began decorating the tree with her sisters, as they always had. Only now the conversation wasn't the same as it used to be, when they would retrieve a forgotten ornament, or find one that they thought had been lost, and all sorts of lovely memories and warm feelings would fill the air.

Now Britt was talking about the tree that she and Robbie and Keira had decorated last night! And Amelia was talking about the one that Matt had helped her carry up the stairs to her living room. And Maddie—who had never put up her own tree before, because she tended to just rely on one of the older sisters for that—was talking about how she and Cole were getting one for his house, and how she was going to bring him into the store for ornaments tomorrow on her day off from the bakery.

Was it so strange that Cora didn't have a tree of her own in her apartment when she had a dozen trees downstairs in her shop?

But the real reason, she knew, why she didn't have a tree of her own, was because this was her tree. The tree in the bay window of her childhood home. The tree that she and her sisters always decorated together, with these special ornaments, in these boxes. The tree with the angel on top.

She blinked back tears that threatened. What could compete with any of that?

Only from the way her sisters were chattering, one thing could. Love. True love. Something that she was yet to find.

"I think I'll go get a refill of that hot chocolate," she said, hoping that no one caught onto the hurt in her voice, but knowing that they probably did. She and her sisters had always been close. Losing their mother had pulled them together, even when some of them, like Britt, had tried to push away. She was back now; her first Christmas in Blue Harbor since she'd left at eighteen.

Only they weren't kids anymore. And even with her here, all Cora could think about was how much things had changed.

"You okay?" Cora knew it was Britt even before she spoke. She knew each of her sisters by the sound of their tread, and Britt had always walked with a clear sense of purpose.

Cora set her mug on the counter and sighed. "I suppose you think I overreacted about the tree topper."

Britt shrugged. "If it means so much to you, why didn't you say anything?"

Cora gave her a pointed look. "You know how pushy Candy can be."

There was no argument there.

"Besides," Cora continued, unable to meet her sister's eye. "I'm starting to feel like I'm the only one who attaches so much meaning to this holiday."

Maddie had appeared over Britt's shoulder by now and scooted past her into the kitchen. "That's not true, Cora. But the holidays always meant the most to you. Without you, I'm not even sure what Christmas would have looked like in the years after we lost Mom."

It was true, Cora knew. Britt was gone for college by then, and Amelia kept busy with practical matters, like tending to the dinners and making sure that Cora and Maddie had everything they needed for school. Their father immersed himself in the orchard, in good hard work. And Maddie clung to the dessert recipes that their mother had made, filling the house with the smells that were as sweet as her memory.

But it was Cora who made sure that they still decorated for Christmas each year. That they still carried out the traditions that had meant so much to their mother, even if she was no longer there to experience it with them.

"You can't expect things to stay the same forever," Britt said gently. "And I'll have you know that for about the first six years of my life, our tree topper was a beautiful glass snowflake that I broke one year, arguing with Amelia over which one of us was going to get to put it up. We got the angel at a craft fair because Mom thought it was more durable with four kids under the roof, all wanting to get their hands on it."

Cora didn't know this story, of course. She would have been too little.

Now, she filled her mug with the cocoa that was still warm in the pot on the stove and swirled it with a candy cane, per tradition.

"I guess I just liked things the way they were," Cora said.

"You mean with Dad sad and lonely and all of us slowly turning into spinsters?" Maddie replied. Then, realizing her misstep, she slapped a hand over her mouth. "Sorry, Cora. You know you'll find someone eventually. There's always Bart. Oh, and you know, there was a guy in the bakery the other day—"

She stopped when she saw Cora give her the long, warning look she always did when Maddie started to get too interested in her love life.

"Bart is a friend," she clarified. "And as for some guy in your bakery, I'm not exactly looking to be set up at the moment. Besides, this is my peak season. I don't have time to think about romance."

It wasn't true. She'd spent entirely too much time during her walk over here thinking of Phil and the fact that he would be staying in town through Christmas.

"You know what Mom always used to say," Amelia chimed in as she joined them through the dining room

entrance and picked up her platter of leftover Thanksgiving sandwiches. "First comes mistletoe!"

They all said it in unison, and Cora laughed, despite her earlier annoyance.

It was true, that above all traditions that their mother loved about this holiday, the part she loved the most was the love. The magic. The way the snow and the lights and the music and the feels all made everything feel more special and romantic.

And that was one tradition that Cora hadn't exactly experienced firsthand. Until now.

4

Unlike her sisters Amelia and Maddie, who closed their establishments on Mondays, Cora remained open seven days a week during the holiday season, knowing that her downtime would come from January through to the spring when tourists started flocking to the lakefront town again. She was happy for the business, especially from Maddie and Cole, who stopped by as promised. Cora had watched them with a funny feeling in her stomach as they walked around the shop, picking out decorations that were clearly the start of a life together, even if it was the early days of their relationship. She wasn't jealous of her sister—no, that wasn't it. It was longing, she realized, for what they had. To find it for herself.

But after waiting all day to see if Phil and Georgie would come in for decorations for their tree, she'd finally turned the sign on the door with a sigh, flicked off the lights, and treated herself to two Christmas movies in her favorite flannel pajamas, and a bowl of cereal for dinner.

Up until now, that kind of night had been something to look forward to after a long day on her feet. But now, after meeting Phil, Cora suddenly itched to get out a little more.

On Tuesday morning, she stopped by Buttercream Bakery for some much-needed coffee. She was pleased to see that the new spot in town was busy on a weekday morning.

She was even more pleased to see how festive Maddie's menu was.

"You might have beaten me when it comes to who has more Christmas in their store," she laughed when Maddie finished up with the customer ahead of her. Cora let her gaze linger on all the treats, most of which had eggnog, candy cane, or spice in their ingredients.

Maddie snorted. "Please, like anyone could top you when it comes to the holidays." She paused, her expression turning momentarily sad. "Well, other than Mom, of course."

Cora gave a wistful smile. Memories of her mother happily hanging a wreath from the front door and putting her candles in each window still made her heart ache nearly as much as it filled it. "She knew how to do it, that was for sure."

"From the roast to the potatoes to the color-coordinated wrapping paper."

"Hey, I thought Santa brought the paper!" Cora teased, but it was true, and she was pleased that Maddie, being the youngest, still remembered that. Each year, their mother picked a few rolls of paper in coordinating prints, and each girl knew whose gifts were for who based on the paper.

It was a tradition she still carried on, wrapping each of her family member's gifts in a different print that suited their personality.

"Maybe that's something you can do with your kids someday," she said. "Now that you and Cole are—"

Maddie pursed her lips, but there was no doubt that she was pleased. "Just dating," she said firmly.

"For now." Cora couldn't deny that it felt good to give Maddie a taste of her own medicine. She'd poked Amelia forever about her romantic life, which had spared Cora until Matt returned to town and Amelia found her happily ever after.

Maddie's cheeks flushed and she swallowed hard as their eyes met. "But speaking of Cole, I've meaning to tell you that—"

She stopped, her expression lifting to one of unabashed excitement as the door jingled and a cold burst of winter air filled the otherwise deliciously warm and spice-scented room.

Maddie leaned in and whispered, "Don't look now, but that guy I was telling you about is back."

Cora stifled a groan. "Is this how it's going to be? Now that you have a boyfriend, you're going to try to fix me up with any man that orders a latte? You're worse than Candy, you know that?"

Maddie pulled back and shrugged. "Suit yourself. But you'll never meet anyone if you sit home every night the way you do."

"I don't sit home *every* night," Cora scoffed. A guilty flush crept up her cheeks when she thought of how she'd spent the night before, not that she'd be letting on. "I mean, not *every* night." Really, was it so bad to be a homebody? She loved her cozy apartment, loved relaxing after a long day. But she supposed it wasn't exactly a good way to meet someone unless it was someone who came into her shop…Her mind drifted back to Phil.

"Not every night, but…most nights?" Maddie gave her a scolding look, but there was a knowing smile teasing her mouth as she tended to Cora's coffee, not bothering to specify the order. Everyone in the Conway family—and probably in town—knew that Cora liked peppermint lattes…every single day of the year.

Because she suspected that her sister was still watching her from the corner of her eye, Cora refused to so much as glance over her shoulder, even if she was a little curious about this man that Maddie was so intent about her meeting.

"Hey," a voice interrupted her thoughts, causing her to jump, and she turned at the sound of it, rich and thick and just smooth enough to make her stand a little straighter.

She smiled in surprise at Phil, who was grinning right back at her. "Hello!" Oh, she really hoped that she didn't say that with the enthusiasm that she felt.

She glanced sidelong at Maddie, who was watching, wide-eyed, with interest.

"So you took me up on the suggestion," she said, wondering if she should really take credit for referring Phil here when this was the only bakery in town and it was breakfast time, after all.

"Oh, this is our second time here," Phil said. He motioned to Georgie, whose nose was pressed against the glass display case as she considered her options. Clearly, this task required utmost concentration.

Phil grinned at Maddie who said, rather cheekily if one were to ask Cora, "Welcome back!"

She gave a little lift of her eyebrow to Cora. Cora did her best to pretend not to notice.

"What can I get for you today?" Maddie asked.

"Two of the cranberry scones, a regular coffee—"

"A candy cane hot chocolate! Please, Dad?" Georgie begged.

After a beat, Phil said, "The hot chocolate." He motioned to Cora's to-go cup. "And whatever she's having."

Cora opened her mouth to protest, but Maddie shot her a look that was brief but clear. One that only they as sisters could read in the eyes.

"Thank you," Cora said, smiling. "You didn't have to."

"Oh, but I did." Phil's brow pulled a little as he handed over some cash. He seemed quiet for a moment, until he said, "If it wasn't for you, I'm not sure that we'd be spending Christmas in this quaint little town."

"You seem to be embracing the idea."

He gave a look that said otherwise. Clearly, he didn't share his daughter's—or her—enthusiasm when it came to the holiday.

"What makes Georgie happy, makes me happy."

"You're a good father," Cora said. She knew one when she saw one; after all, she had firsthand experience with the best man a girl could have ever had, especially after they lost their mother.

Phil didn't look convinced. "Depends on the day."

She grinned, trying her best to avoid meeting Maddie's eye, who was no doubt memorizing every word of this exchange to report back to their older sisters. "And what do you have planned while you're in town?"

"Other than decorating our new tree?" Phil shrugged. "What do people do in town for Christmas?"

Maddie made a big show of clearing her throat but feigned innocence as she handed Phil his scones. Cora could have swatted her.

If her sister thought that Phil was fishing around for a date, she was probably mistaken. The man was just looking for a little company. Or some insight about the holidays from the town's expert.

Still, Maddie might be a little pushy, but she also had her best interest at heart. Cora pulled in a breath, wondering if she was being forward by what she wanted to say next, or just plain friendly. Friendly, she decided. After all, she would have said the same thing to any newcomer to town. It just so happened that this one fell under the dangerously attractive and single and likable category.

"The same things we've always done! The annual tree lighting is this Friday night," she said. "It's a lot of fun. They light up the tree and sing carols. Pretty much the entire town comes out for it."

Georgie gasped. "Can we go, Daddy?"

"I don't see why not," he said. He looked at Cora. "Thanks. And…I imagine I'll be seeing you before then, too."

Cora felt her cheeks heat as she questioned his implication. "At the shop," she finally said, wanting to shake her other thoughts clear. Of course, they would be in for decorations like they'd said at the tree lot. Maybe there was nothing more to it than that.

But when they collected their hot drinks and waved good-bye, Cora felt some hesitation from Phil, like there was something more he wanted to say to her, and then changed his mind. She lingered behind, not only because she didn't want to look like she was following them out, but because it was fairly clear from the way Maddie was tossing looks her way that a postmortem was in order.

Maddie tipped her head toward the kitchen door as her assistant slipped behind the counter. Cora checked the time. She supposed she could spare a few minutes. And she couldn't exactly contain this feeling that something magical was happening this Christmas, right here in this sleepy little town that she loved so much.

"Cora! That's the guy that I was telling you about," Maddie hissed as she closed the door behind them.

Cora hadn't even considered the possibility and now she looked sheepishly at her sister. Damn. Would she be forced to admit that she was a little open to love, especially with Phil, who had clearly already won her younger sister's stamp of approval?

She swept her eyes over the kitchen, where canisters of flour and sugar were clearly labeled, and the counter held a mixing bowl and several baking sheets. Maddie immediately began rolling out dough after washing her hands.

"How do you know him?"

"Oh, he came into the shop," Cora said dismissively. Really, she realized with a sinking heart, there was nothing more to it than that. Only it felt like there was. Like something kept bringing Phil back to the store, or in her path.

But then, that was small-town living for you.

"And?" Maddie reached for a cookie cutter and began stamping the dough. "Where is he from? What's his story?"

"I don't know, really. I don't even know his last name," Cora replied with a sigh. "All I know is that he's here through the holidays."

"That's weeks from now!" Maddie exclaimed. "A lot can happen in a few weeks, you know."

Yes, Cora knew that it could. Maddie was proof of that. She'd fallen in love with her contractor right here in this very kitchen while he was building her dream bakery.

But could something like that happen to her?

She thought of what her mother always used to say about the magic of Christmas and decided that it was entirely possible. Especially at Christmas.

*

In between screening half a dozen voicemails and leaving twice as many in return for his staff back in the office, Phil listened as Georgie talked about how she planned to decorate the tree for the entire drive home. Home meaning his grandparents' summer home. In all honesty, Phil didn't really know what constituted as home anymore. It wasn't his condo in the city; Georgie had drawn some light to that, made him realize that while it was functional and convenient, and even spacious, it was only a place to live.

And it wouldn't be for long. He had already found someone to lease it for two years, the expected duration of his time in Europe. Visits back to the States would be infrequent, and there was a corporate apartment he could use for that.

He supposed that home base would revert to his childhood home now; neither of his parents spent much time there. His father was working, and his mother was always busy with a committee or theatre tickets or museum event. The city brownstone that he'd grown up in had felt large and empty, with dinners mostly eaten out at restaurants, the kitchen always spotless.

Here in Blue Harbor, his grandparents' house had felt foreign, small by comparison, and a bit rundown, even all those years ago. Now, as he opened the door and flicked on the lights, he knew that if he was going to make an easy sale of it, he'd need to at least tend to a few minor repairs. It would likely sell to someone like him, he supposed, someone within driving distance who was looking for a vacation getaway.

Only that was where the comparison stopped. Phil didn't do vacations. Phil worked.

He set the bags from the hardware store on the kitchen counter, knowing that he should have stopped by the

Christmas shop before coming back to the house. By the terms of Cora's lease, she was entitled to a thirty-day written notice, and as the executor of his grandparents' estate, he'd hoped to tie this up by year-end. He supposed an extra week wouldn't change the outcome of the sale. When he'd briefly spoken over the phone to the real estate agent in town about listing the two properties, he was told that both would likely sell when people began thinking about warmer weather.

The property on Main would likely be turned into an inn, much like the handful of others that lined the street. According to the real estate agent, there were always a few buyers circling the area, watching and waiting for an opportunity to pop up. Phil vaguely remembered the way his grandmother would dream of turning the property into a B&B—something that made his father snort, knowing the kind of capital it would take to make that happen.

Sure, his grandparents weren't rich by any means, but they weren't uncomfortable, either. They worked hard as bookkeepers for neighboring businesses, and Phil's grandfather had made the choice to downsize to the cottage for less pressure and a simpler life. And more time to fish, he always pointed out. Oh, how that made Phil's father roll his eyes. That house on Main had been his home, moving out of it was something he'd never quite forgiven his parents for. He wanted more out of life. More for himself than he could find in Blue Harbor.

The house on Main Street would be an easy sell, Phil knew, but the cottage would be harder to part with for his grandparents, which was why Phil hadn't shared the details of how he planned to handle their affairs. They trusted him to do the right thing, and that was to unload the properties. His grandparents would never return to Blue Harbor at this stage of their lives, and there was no chance that Phil's father would either. There was nothing to hold onto here.

Other than memories.

Phil shook away the thoughts. This was a time for action. There was no room for emotion to creep in. This was his wheelhouse. He knew how to focus, get the job done, not let his mind wander down paths of different scenarios. When something made sense, he did it. There were always casualties; it came with the territory. It had just never bothered him until now.

Tomorrow he would tell Cora the news. Surely, he had delivered worse news before—laying off hundreds, even thousands of employees at a time. It was part of his job: never pleasant, but necessary.

Even right before Christmas.

Nonsense. Since when did he care about the holiday?

His mind made up, today he would tend to the house, and he would start with the easy projects, like the loose doorknobs.

"I didn't know you knew how to use a screwdriver, Daddy." Georgie looked amused as she ate her scone at the kitchen table, watching him across the room.

"Well, then you learned something new about me today," he said with a grin. He hesitated, remembering how it was his grandfather who had introduced him to the wonders of a toolbox out in the very garage where his car was now parked. They'd spent hours out there, tinkering with the boat, or little projects around the house, and Phil had loved the one-on-one time, something he'd never experienced with his own father.

And still didn't. No matter how hard he tried.

Phil looked at the tool in his hand now as a thought took hold. He raised an eyebrow at his daughter. "Do *you* know how to use a screwdriver?"

Georgie thought about it for a moment. "I don't think so."

"Come here," he said, gesturing her over. "I'll teach you."

Georgie looked as pleased as he felt when she set down her scone and walked over to where he stood at the powder room door. He handed her the tool and walked her through the process, slowly, carefully, until she had tightened the screws.

"Look at that!" he exclaimed.

His grandfather would be proud. He'd make a point to tell him, next time he saw him.

Phil's stomach twisted on that thought. He wasn't sure when he would see his grandparents again, now that he considered it. He rarely visited the home they were in, and he hadn't factored that into the timeline between now and his move.

"When are we going to decorate the tree?" Georgie asked.

"Soon," Phil replied.

"Mom always decorates the tree the day she gets it," Georgie continued. "And she hangs stockings."

Stockings. Shoot. Right.

"And she puts a wreath on the door, and she sometimes puts a candy cane in my lunch box."

He knew that he couldn't fault Michelle and that everything that Georgie said was true. Michelle was a good mother. And everything that she had said was true, too.

He hadn't been there for Georgie in the past. Hadn't shown up at the big events, hadn't treasured the small milestones. Hadn't seen the value in a sit-down family dinner or conversation about how they'd spent their day. He'd focused on the big house, the top-of-the-line swing set, the private music lessons, and the expensive school.

He'd tried to give his daughter a good life, and now his child preferred to spend her time with her mother. Preferred to spend her holidays without him.

And when he stopped to think about it, who could blame her?

Hadn't he, after all, once longed for more time in this very town, with simple pleasures that only his grandparents had provided?

He reached for his coffee, but found, much like his excitement for expanding his business opportunities overseas, that it had gone cold.

5

By Friday, Georgie had made it clear that she couldn't wait to get the tree decorated any longer. She had made some paper garland and other ornaments with supplies she had found around the house. Phil had searched the attic for the decorations that had belonged to his grandparents, but that only revealed dust bunnies and a cedar chest with a yellowing wedding gown that still managed to spark a gasp of delight from Georgie.

"I guess that Great-Grandma and Grandpa didn't like to celebrate Christmas either," Georgie said with a shrug.

That wasn't true, and he opened his mouth to tell her so, but thought the better of it. Georgie was restless, tired of sitting around while he tended to work calls and emails, and the day was getting on. Soon it would be dark, and the provisions that he'd picked up last weekend were running low. He'd have to hit the frozen food aisle or find a restaurant in town for dinner.

If it was just him, like it usually was, he'd be happy with another frozen pizza, or even a decent sandwich, but Georgie had made it clear that this wouldn't suffice, and he wasn't up for an argument. Technically, he had enough work to stay busy for hours more, but Phil supposed it would be nice to stretch his legs and get into town, and the least he could do, he supposed, was throw some business toward the poor owner of the holiday shop. And give her fair warning.

"Let's head into town," he said before he could change his mind. He closed his laptop firmly, deciding that it was really just a distraction from the business at hand. He'd come to town to wrap up his grandparents' estate and that was exactly what he needed to tend to at the moment. Besides, unlike his other projects, he didn't have any assistance on this one, or backup. If he wanted to get things in Blue Harbor cleared up before Christmas, he'd have to handle it on his own.

With that in mind, he drove them into town and parked the car near the square, where concession stands were already being set up for the tree lighting ceremony.

"Look how big that tree is!" Georgie pointed in awe at a giant spruce standing tall in the center of a snow-covered park.

"I don't think they bought that at the tree lot," Phil replied, and even he was impressed by the size of the tree. He didn't know what he'd been expecting, but it almost gave the tree in Chicago a running. All this time, he'd assumed his memory had been distorted by childish exaggeration—making his experiences here out to be better than they actually were. But Blue Harbor was exactly like he remembered, and he wasn't so sure how he felt about that.

It was easier to think of it all as a fantasy, rather than a possibility.

"I wonder if Cora gets to decorate the tree?" Georgie asked, interrupting his thoughts.

Phil helped his daughter maneuver an icy patch on the sidewalk as they neared the store. "You'll have to ask her."

That was, if she still spoke to them after he delivered the news. He'd decided to just get right to it. No more stalling. Surely, as a shop owner, she'd understand. And it wasn't like he was putting her out of business—something that was often the case. She just had to move her merchandise to a different storefront. Really, this was no big deal at all. A minor inconvenience at best.

He'd spotted at least one or two empty stores off Main Street when they went to the bakery the other day. Perfectly viable options. And didn't her sisters work there, down near the lakefront? It would be a win-win. Really, she might be happy to have a fresh new space.

Jingle bells jangled when Georgie pushed open the shop door, welcoming them to the warm and heavily scented space. Each time he came here, the place felt more crammed. Packed from the floor to the ceiling with seasonal dust catchers that would all be packed up come New Year's.

He looked down at his daughter, whose eyes twinkled as she looked around the room. It was worth it, he decided. Work could wait—at least until she went to bed tonight. But this time with his daughter…it was long overdue.

Georgie wasted no time in starting to fill her basket, reaching for anything and everything that was pretty, sparkling, and breakable.

"Please be careful," he warned, realizing the hypocrisy in that statement. Here he was, telling his daughter to protect the store, when he was responsible for shutting it down?

Or at least he would be, when he finally told Cora what he should have said the very first day he walked in, back when this was just a random property he wanted no further ties to, not a place that had become so important to his daughter in a short matter of time.

Not a place where Cora worked. Looking just as pretty as always, he couldn't help noticing.

Today her sweater was cream and soft looking, with her thick hair falling loose at her shoulders. She smiled when she saw him across the room, and motioned that she'd be right with him.

No rush, he wanted to mouth. But that wasn't exactly true. He couldn't stall forever.

While she tended to the customers, he walked deeper into the store, monitoring Georgie from a distance, taking in the packed rooms of the old Victorian home that she had filled by theme, it would seem. And oh, was it stuffed. From the floors to the ceilings, where even from the rafters there seemed to hang wreaths and lights and tinsel.

"Isn't it wonderful?" Georgie exclaimed as she passed him her basket and went to fetch another.

Phil looked down at the items that rested in the basket in his hands. Wonderful wasn't a word that he would use. Expensive, yes. Frivolous, sure.

A giant commercial enterprise that plenty of people seemed to feed into from the looks of the place. One thing was for certain; Cora wasn't hurting for business.

But then, Christmas was only weeks away.

His stomach tightened at the thought. In less than a month he'd be gone, overseas.

And Georgie still didn't know.

And just like the news he was yet to deliver to Cora, he wasn't sure why he was holding back. Michelle had said it was his responsibility to tell Georgie. His news to share. And what was really so different? He could always fly back for a visit, meaning that whether it was an ocean dividing them or the prairie states, not much had changed. And it was for work.

It was business. Just like unloading this shop.

"Everything okay?"

He turned to see Cora standing beside him, her cheeks flushed, but a look of concern crinkling her lovely blue eyes. He nodded, grateful for the distraction because distraction it was. From the stress of parenthood, from the memories he was trying to banish being back in this place. But she was also a distraction from what he'd come to do here. What he had to do.

"I see you're going to have a very pink tree!" She motioned to the items in his basket with a laugh.

"Not exactly traditional," he said ruefully, but Cora just shook her head.

"Everyone has their own traditions, however unconventional. Pink ornaments will be yours." She smiled at this, and despite everything, he joined her. "That is, unless you have other traditions?"

He shook his head. "Nope. Christmas was never a big deal for my family."

Cora's eyes widened in surprise. "Well, it's a very big deal for mine! We have special activities planned all season long, started as far back as I can remember. My mother would always make the smallest parts of the season special, beginning with the decorations. We came to love all of it so much, that we couldn't even change up the dessert come Christmas Eve." She laughed.

"My mom always makes a cake for Christmas," Georgie announced.

Phil had forgotten that, but it was true. Usually, he was working too late to taste any—she would send the leftovers home to her sister and three boys. Georgie would already be in bed, and the presents were already wrapped and under the tree. He was always there for the opening, of course. The swift destruction of paper that no doubt took hours to wrap.

So inefficient.

"We always have cranberry pie, and only for Christmas," Cora said, smiling wistfully. "It's nice to have something to look forward to all year, I think. Something to rely on?"

She blinked at him as if waiting for confirmation. He opened his mouth to say something—anything—that might get them on the subject of the store itself—but he was jostled to the side by an elderly couple.

He moved toward the wall for more space. And privacy. Now was as good a time as any to broach the subject of selling this old building. Best to get it over with. Really, he'd never had a problem conducting such straightforward business before. But then, it was never personal before.

"Daddy, look at that angel!" Georgie said, coming up to them. She was pointing at an angel on the tree next to where he stood, and he craned his neck to look at it. Old and used, if anyone were to ask him.

"That one is not for sale, I'm afraid," Cora said. "Actually, that angel was one of our traditions. I have three sisters, you see, and each year we would argue over whose turn it was to put the angel on the top branch."

"Strange tradition. Arguing?" Exactly what Phil didn't understand about the holiday. From where he stood, it just brought out the worst in people. His mother used it as an excuse to drink too much, to turn charitable events into social scenes. And his father saw it as an excuse to hide, to work more. But there was no arguing. They were never all together long enough to argue.

Cora tipped her head. Her eyes were bright as she stared up at the angel. "You'd think so, but that angel brings back some of my happiest Christmas memories, and we all need some of those."

Phil's smile felt tight. He had one happy Christmas memory. Just one. And he'd tried his best to forget it.

"Why isn't it on your tree then?" Georgie asked.

"Good question." Cora sighed heavily. "My family grew up and changed, and so did this tradition. I love Christmas the most, they all say, well, other than my mother, but I got it from her. So I brought the angel here, where she can always be with me and remind me of why I love this holiday, and this store so much."

Phil felt his mouth go dry. He could swear the temperature in the room just went up a couple of degrees.

"Well, we should probably let you get back to your customers," he said. He took Georgie's second basket from her hand. Normally he'd wade through the stuff. Half of it was dust-catchers that would either break or be forgotten come the day they took down the tree. The money would be better off in a high-interest college savings account, practically speaking.

But he was about to single-handedly shut this place down. The least he could do was buy a few ornaments.

Cora rang them up, and Phil couldn't help but gape at the figure she told him. Another problem with a small store like this. Most people would only buy one or two things at these prices, and now that he looked around, he realized that while the store was filled, most people were doing just that. He'd taken over many companies like this. Bought them out, restructured, set them up for a more successful future. Maybe he could share a little wisdom with Cora—guide her to a better path. A different path, technically.

"This is a big space," he started, feeling her out.

"I need it for all my merchandise!" She laughed good-naturedly. "My sisters probably think I should buy less, sell what I have, but, well, I love it, I'm afraid. I'm my own best customer."

Despite himself, he smiled. She loved what she did. And better—or worse—she loved where worked. She was a hard worker—something they had in common.

But it probably stopped right there.

"So you've always been in this space? You didn't grow into it?"

Cora smiled. "Always here. The people I lease it from just love Christmas."

Phil managed a polite nod but his jaw felt tense. It was true that his grandparents had loved Christmas. Still did, far as he knew. They fed into the fantasy of it all, much like their lifestyle in Blue Harbor—laid-back, carefree, every day felt like a vacation. But that wasn't real life. And it wasn't his life.

And in time, it was easier to forget the music and the lights and the joy that had come with that one perfect Christmas.

He realized, however, that it was Cora's life. And that she probably wouldn't be very willing to give it up.

"They were so supportive of me starting a shop like this that they gave me a great deal on the space, and it went a long way in enabling me to go through with it!"

Phil knew that the rent was low, but he'd assumed that was because this was a small town, not a big city where retail space went for a premium price tag. Now he shifted uneasily on his feet. He hadn't considered that rents elsewhere in Blue Harbor might exceed Cora's budget.

"Plus, this place has so much character," Cora went on. "I love the winding rooms, how I can really get creative with the entire space. At Halloween, I even have a haunted house room."

She rubbed her hands together for Georgie, who lapped it up, excitedly. "Can we come back for Halloween, Dad?"

"I think you're with your mother for Halloween," he said, realizing that next October would have been his Halloween with Georgie. His first since the divorce, and only because she was moving back to the Midwest.

Right when he was leaving.

Georgie pouted, while Cora finished wrapping their items. She tossed in a candy cane from the jar on the counter, giving Georgie a little wink.

That did the trick. His daughter's smile was back, and as for Phil…his resolve was gone.

This was a conversation that couldn't be had in front of his daughter. Or with a line of people forming behind him.

He paid with cash again, eager not to reveal his last name and connection to this store just yet, and sideswiped the snow globe on the crowded counter with the bag.

"Careful, Daddy!" Georgie warned. "My Christmas wish came true," Georgie said, looking suddenly at Cora. "Did yours?"

Cora gave Georgie a little smile. "We'll see."

Phil was in a cold sweat by now. The store was stifling, his coat was heavy, and his guilt was strong.

"I think that the tree lighting is starting soon," he told Georgie, even though he had originally hoped she'd be too excited about the new ornaments to bother with seeing a tree in town all lit up. But anything would be better than standing here, face to face with the woman whose life he would soon be responsible for ruining.

It was different when he dealt with businesses, company takeovers. He didn't have to face the people. He didn't have to know their stories.

"Oh, look at the time!" Cora's eyes went to the Nutcracker-themed coo-coo clock on the wall. "It's just about time to close up shop!"

"You can come with us if you want," Georgie said.

"Oh, Georgie," Phil said urgently. "I'm sure that Cora has her family waiting for her. They have their traditions."

Cora's cheeks flushed. "It's true we do, but…"

But? He held his breath, wanting to get away from this woman almost as much as he knew he really should continue their conversation, lay it all out there.

"Well, my sisters all have boyfriends now," Cora replied, with a shrug. "I was going to meet some of my cousins…but…maybe I'll look for you. I happen to know they have really good cider at this event," she whispered faux conspiratorially. "And my cousin Jenna is the head of the Christmas choir. They always put on quite a show."

"Sounds like a plan," Phil said, backing away to the door.

A good plan, actually. A nice plan, by all accounts. But not the original plan. Not at all.

*

Well, that was smooth.

Cora rolled her eyes skyward as she closed the door and turned the lock. Her eyes met the ball of mistletoe and she tightened her lips. She'd never get a Christmas kiss at this rate! Every time she ran into Phil, she was all nervous and jittery. She should be grateful that Natalie had already left to take her daughter to the tree lighting event, or Cora was pretty sure that she would have been on the receiving end of a lecture on how to flirt. As a single mother, Natalie wasn't shy about her desire to settle down and find a father figure for her young child.

She wasn't shy in general.

Whereas Cora…She pulled in a breath.

Tonight she would have to do better.

Tonight. Her stomach rolled with fresh nerves and she dashed up the back stairs and into her bathroom to touch up her hair from a long day's work.

Bundled in her warmest coat and softest scarf, she headed down Main Street a few minutes later. Even from her building, she could see that the town square was already bustling. The annual tree lighting was one of her favorite traditions in town; the large, illuminated tree was the centerpiece of the annual Winter Carnival.

Cora didn't care what people said. Blue Harbor may be a summer destination for most, but in her opinion, nothing could top the tried-and-true holiday festivities that were a hallmark year after year.

Except maybe a newcomer to town…

Her eyes somehow fell immediately on Phil and Georgie when she approached the snow-covered square, but rather than approach them right away, she decided to say a quick hello to her sisters while she was still alone. Maddie had already been suggestive enough for one week, and tonight she didn't need anyone ogling her or teasing her if she was enjoying a few minutes of Phil's company. Which she hoped to do, very much.

Amelia and Maddie had decided to join forces for the snacks stand, while Britt and Robbie were handling the cider stand, with mulled wine also on the menu. It was just like old times, seeing Amelia and Maddie together, and Cora felt a warm glow fill her chest.

Maybe her sisters were right. They'd each moved on and grown, but ultimately, everything was still very much the same.

"Don't look now, but—" Maddie started, but Cora just shook her head.

"I already saw him," she said, hoping that she could retain a neutral expression.

"Saw who?" Amelia perked up with interest. Even though they were standing near one of the many bonfires set up as warming stations, she shivered in her coat.

"Oh, just a very attractive single father who happens to be staying in town until Christmas." Maddie waggled her eyebrows. "Or possibly longer."

Cora's heart flip-flopped. "Did he say that?"

Maddie pointed at her. "See! I knew you liked him! But no, he didn't say anything. I was just guessing. I mean, if he's in town for a month, who says he can't stay longer?"

Cora tried to hide the disappointment she felt. "He's in town for the holidays, Maddie. He lives in Chicago. He made it very clear that he has a big job to get back to. And I know that his daughter spends most of her time with her mother, too. Besides, I've only bumped into him a few times. It's not like he has sought me out. Let's not get ahead of ourselves here."

"Point him out," Amelia ordered, clearly ignoring Cora's excuse, and Maddie all too happily obliged. Craning her neck, Amelia nodded approvingly. "Very cute. And so is the little girl. So what are you doing standing around talking to us, Cora? Go over there!"

Cora shifted the weight on her feet, feeling the snow crunch beneath her boots. "I will, in a minute. I was just...giving them time to settle in."

"To settle in? Or to have one of the many single and searching women in town swoop in?" Maddie tsked under her breath. "And here comes one now."

Cora looked over in alarm, and was almost relieved to see that it was just Candy.

"Well, now you have to go over there," Amelia said, laughing.

"You need to save the poor man," Maddie agreed.

"Fine. I did promise Georgie that I'd get her a hot cider," Cora said, pulling in a breath for courage.

"Did you now?" Maddie replied, and even though the great tree had not yet been lit, her eyes twinkled merrily.

Not exactly, but it was enough of a promise to give Cora a little courage. She couldn't let a little girl down, especially at Christmastime.

Cora thrust her hands deep into the pockets of her coat and trekked across the square to where Phil was standing, listening to Candy talk with full animation.

Seeing her, Candy nearly squealed, and before Cora could brace herself, she was enveloped in a long, squishy hug.

"We were *just* talking about you!" Candy cried joyfully, when she finally released Cora, causing her to nearly lose her footing.

Cora took a step backward, steadying herself, and flashed a glance at Phil, who looked appropriately amused. Cora, however, was not.

"All good things, I hope?" Only she needn't have asked. Candy was forever singing the praises of the Conway girls. It was endearing, she knew, and it was probably why their father loved her so much, but Cora wasn't so sure how she felt about Candy pushing her on a man she had just met.

"Of course!" Candy gave her an exaggerated wink and giggled loudly. "I was delighted to hear that you and Phil already know each other!"

That was a stretch, but because Cora didn't feel the need to explain, she said nothing. "I was going to see if Georgie wanted to try some of that cider? It's nice and warm, and the line is already pretty long."

She glanced over her shoulder, where sure enough, the queue was wrapped in both directions, and Britt and Robbie stood side-by-side, working quickly.

"Oh! I *see*!" Candy's eyes were round. "Well, don't let me get in the way! I was just about to run and find Denny. He got to talking to Robbie's parents, and when I saw this tall, dark, and handsome stranger over here, I couldn't resist the urge to introduce myself." She honked loudly, chuckling at herself, and Cora saw Georgie frown in confusion.

"How about that cider?" Cora whispered to her.

Georgie nodded happily and Candy mercifully jogged away, looking back a few times to give a less than discreet thumbs-up sign.

Cora closed her eyes briefly. She was happy in the dark that Phil probably couldn't make out the flush in her cheeks that now heated her more than her wool scarf.

"That's my father's girlfriend," she explained as they began walking toward the stand. "She's mostly harmless, but certainly not shy."

"Your dad has a girlfriend?" Georgie looked at her with interest as they joined the back of the line.

Cora sighed. He had been alone for more than fourteen years after her mother died, and none of them had even considered the possibility that he would find love again, much less want it. Yet here he was, happily attending the holiday event with Candy, who was an increasingly permanent fixture in their lives.

"My mom passed away a long time ago," she said, seeing the sympathy pass through Phil's eyes. No need to be a downer just now, not when it was one of Blue Harbor's most festive nights of the year. "And yes, my dad has a girlfriend. And I should warn you that she works at the café next to the bakery, along with one of my older sisters."

"Do you know everyone in town?" Phil laughed.

Cora looked at him quizzically. "Of course! That's small-town living for you. My entire family lives in town. Over there is my cousin Gabby. She owns the flower shop. And her sister is a piano teacher. She'll be performing tonight with the carolers. Now her other sister moved away, so I guess not every one of my family members lives in town right now." And she was babbling. Cora was happy to see that they were nearly at the head of the line now. "And just to warn you, that's my oldest sister, Britt, serving the cider."

"Conway," Phil observed, reading the sign. "Family business?"

Cora grinned. "Of course. Best fruit and wine in the county. Best in the state, really."

"Best cider too, I hope," Georgie said, watching as someone passed them with a steaming cup.

"The very best," Cora said with a smile. She introduced Phil and Georgie to Britt and Robbie when their turn finally came, averting as best she could the look of curious interest that came over her eldest sister.

"Robbie has a daughter a little younger than you," Britt told Georgie. "If you guys are in town through the weekend, you girls could make cookies together at the gingerbread event."

"Gingerbread event?" Phil looked confused.

Cora explained, "Each year the town comes together and makes a big gingerbread house or village. It's held in the town hall basement, where there's a big industrial kitchen for various town events. But my sister Amelia who owns the café is technically in charge this year, and Maddie is helping."

"I don't remember that..." Phil said, and Cora looked at him sharply.

"So you've been to Blue Harbor for Christmas before?"

Phil looked away, evasive. "Just once. We mostly came in the summer."

He didn't elaborate, and Cora didn't want to press. She was talking too much already. Out of practice. Not that she'd ever had much practice. A few boyfriends here and there, nothing that ever really stuck.

Nothing like what her parents had. Or like her sisters had now found.

"It's been going on for about twenty years now, maybe more." Meaning by her rough calculation, Phil hadn't been to Blue Harbor for Christmas since he was about Georgie's age. Sure enough, a sign for the event was tacked to one of several tree trunks and she motioned to it now.

"I want to decorate a gingerbread house! That sounds like fun!" Georgie said.

"Then I guess that means we'll go," Phil said, and Cora couldn't resist the way her heart tugged with excitement.

"Great, I'll be there, too," Britt said. "We all will, right, Cora?" She gave her a meaningful look.

Obviously, Cora had intended to go. She never missed a tradition!

"See you then," Phil said pleasantly as they walked away.

Cora wondered how many yards they had to walk before Britt whipped out her phone and began texting their other two sisters across the town square. Two yards, she hedged. Three at most.

"This cider is the best! You were right!" Georgie said, smiling.

"I used to help make it when I was younger," Cora confided. "The orchard has been around for generations, and now my sister Britt runs it."

"And offering cider here at the tree lighting? Is that new?"

"Oh, no, that's tradition," Cora answered.

Phil seemed to peer at her. "You really like your traditions around here."

"Who doesn't? Isn't that what makes the holidays so great?" Cora stared at him, only to come to realize that he didn't seem to share her enthusiasm. Still, he was here, and he had agreed to the cookie baking. There was hope for him yet.

And maybe, hope for her too.

"We still haven't decorated our tree," Georgie complained, giving a meaningful look at her father.

"Well, you did just buy the ornaments today," Cora pointed out.

Georgie's face lit up. "Can you come over and help us decorate? Please? You do such a good job! You're like…an expert."

Cora laughed, but her cheeks had warmed and she didn't dare look Phil in the eye. "I will admit that I am quite an expert when it comes to Christmas."

"Cora might have to work," Phil said gently, eliciting a groan of disappointment from Georgie.

"It is a very busy time of year for the shop," Cora agreed. "But I find time to keep things balanced and still enjoy the season." She could practically hear her sisters applauding her for that smooth line!

"It seems to do well," Phil observed.

Cora didn't want to admit just how slow her post-Christmas months could be until the tourism picked up again in the spring. Or that she had ventured into Halloween and Thanksgiving holidays as a way to grow her revenue. Her sisters were probably right: she should stop buying new merchandise until she sold what she had. But she loved keeping things fresh and exciting. Could she help it if she was passionate?

"So you could come after work?" Georgie said hopefully. "I could wait another day. I've already waited all week." She slid her father a rueful look, and Cora started to laugh.

"We really don't want to put Cora out," Phil insisted. "She probably has plans tomorrow night, honey."

He glanced up at her, and Cora's mind went blank. Plans? Not unless you called a date with her television and a Christmas movie plans. And she had been looking forward to that. It was part of her traditions and all. But she wouldn't mind changing things if she had the opportunity to spend a little more time with Georgie. And Phil.

"I wouldn't want to impose," she said politely. "Decorating a tree is a very personal experience, after all." When both looked at her in confusion, she continued, "It's usually something that each family has a way of doing. Certain rituals."

"We don't have rituals," Georgie said. "My dad doesn't usually have a tree."

Phil tossed up his hands. "Guilty as charged."

"And why is it that you have no tree?" Cora tilted her head, waiting with a smile.

He shrugged. "Too much work."

"Too much work or too little time?"

"Both." He grinned. "I run a private equity company. There's always something to do."

"So you help struggling companies?" she asked, trying to imagine him in a suit and a conference room every day. Sure, he seemed a little out of place here in Blue Harbor in his sleek wool jacket instead of a parka and those fancy leather gloves, but she couldn't quite imagine this other life of his.

But then, she struggled to imagine any life outside of Blue Harbor. It was all she had ever known or wanted to know.

"Something like that," he said. "But when it comes to all this...Christmas stuff, well, I'm afraid that this is all sort of out of my element."

Clearly. And she was an expert, after all. "Well, I'm happy to help—"

"Please!"

"Only if you're sure…" Phil's eyes looked torn. "No pressure."

"We live in the blue cottage on Forest Road," Georgie interrupted, and for some reason, a strange look took over Phil's face. He opened his mouth and then closed it, growing quiet.

Cora frowned. She knew that house. In a town this small, you tended to know every house that you pedaled past on your bike day after day, and the blue cottage on Forest was no exception, especially because it belonged to the Keatons.

"The Keaton house?" She'd been renting her own building from the Keaton family for years.

"Err…yes." Phil blinked at her slowly. Georgie opened her mouth to say something, but Phil added, "We're, uh…staying there for the month."

"Oh!" Cora grinned, warming at the connection between them. Small world. She didn't even know the family had finally decided to rent out the place, as most seasonal people did. Still, since the Keatons had moved away last winter, it made sense, she supposed.

Another happy coincidence, or maybe, just maybe a sign. Phil and Georgie kept passing into her life, and the more that their lives were brought together, the more that Cora couldn't quite think it was just pure coincidence.

Maybe, it was a little bit of fate. Or a little bit of that Christmas magic that had finally come her way.

6

Before turning the sign on the door the next morning, Cora tossed on her coat and trekked down the street to Gabby's flower shop, knowing that her cousin would have her order ready and waiting.

Like every other shop in town, the flower shop was decked out for the holidays, with a fresh pine wreath on the door and poinsettias and ivy arrangements all over the small room. Also like Cora, Gabby lived right above her shop, only unlike Cora, she had to walk outside to access her own front door.

"Sometimes I feel like I live at work," she complained today, shivering as she turned on the lights.

"You didn't put on a coat?" Cora stopped to smell some lovely red roses, knowing that by the first week of January, her store would have its share of heart and cupid and rose-themed decorations to balance out the Christmas stock she displayed all year round.

"The doors are side by side!" Gabby brushed away her concern. "Besides, I have a feeling I will get all too warm and tingly hearing about your new beau."

Cora laughed. "My new beau? You mean the one with the little girl?" She didn't dare say his name, or she'd really risk stoking that fire in her cousin. Clearly, one of her sisters had been talking last night at the tree lighting.

"Yes, that one!" Gabby said excitedly. "I didn't want to interrupt you guys last night, but it looked like you were really hitting it off."

Ah, spotted then. She could easily turn the conversation to Jenna's choir, who had put on their best performance yet, in her opinion, but Cora supposed there was no use in denying it, even if there wasn't anything to necessarily tell.

"It's nothing. He's come into the shop a few times—"

"A few times?" Gabby looked at her pointedly. "If the same man kept showing in my shop, I'd assume he had good reason."

Cora grinned, not wanting to get her hopes up too much.

"And then you just happened to do to the tree lighting together?"

"We *were* having a nice time," Cora confessed with a grin.

And then, because she couldn't quite resist, she let Gabby grab her by the hands and squeal, just like when they were kids again and had been asked out on a first date.

"Okay, coffee first, then tell me everything," Gabby said matter-of-factly, immediately snapping them back to adulthood.

Cora considered the time, but then she saw that she had half an hour before her shop opened. Technically she could stay for one cup of coffee and still have time to get the store lights turned on—something that wasn't always a brief task when you owned a holiday shop. Natalie wouldn't be in until ten today.

"His name is Phil," she said.

"Phil? Just Phil?" Gabby expertly started her small coffeepot that was plugged in near her computer.

Cora frowned for a moment and then shrugged. "I guess I haven't caught his last name yet."

"Well, you'd better, in case you marry him!" Gabby shook her head. "What if his last name is something really hard to spell? Or what if it rhymes with your name?"

"Then I'll keep Conway," Cora replied, then, catching herself, she scolded, "And who said I'm going to marry the guy?"

Gabby shrugged. "You never know. Things have to start somewhere, don't they?"

It was true, but still, Cora didn't want to get her hopes up too much. Besides, she didn't even know him yet—and not knowing his last name was proof of that.

"What does this Phil do?" Gabby asked as she prepared the coffee machine at the back of her workspace.

"He's a businessman. Very successful, I gather," Cora said, unable to hide her smile.

She was rewarded with a knowing look from Gabby. Yes, this guy was a major catch. But it wasn't necessarily a slam dunk.

"He's divorced," she told Gabby.

"So he's not afraid of commitment," Gabby said, ever the optimist.

Cora had to laugh. "He's from Chicago. He's only in town through Christmas."

There. That should sober her cousin, and get her off her back a bit. Still, she had to admit that it was fun to get excited about something, and it was always easier to let her guard down with her cousins rather than her sisters, especially the older two.

Gabby mulled this over as she plucked two mugs from a lower cabinet under her counter. Cora spotted neat rows of glass vases in all shapes and sizes.

"He…he invited me to decorate his tree tonight."

Gabby did a poor job of hiding her smile. "Did he now?"

"Yes," Cora said, flushing. "He did. But it was only because Georgie asked…"

"And Georgie is the little girl, I assume." Gabby shook her head and slid a mug of steaming coffee to Cora. "Don't sell yourself short, cousin. He would have made up an excuse if he didn't want you there. For all you know, he set her up to it."

Cora really laughed now. "You read way too many romance novels, you know."

Gabby shrugged good-naturedly. "Professional hazard. I'm in the business of the simplest form of a sweeping romantic gesture."

"And I'm in the business of Christmas."

"Yes, but that never stopped you from enjoying it in the past," Gabby said. "And you know that when people fall in love at Christmas, it's the most romantic time of all."

Cora rolled her eyes, even though she knew this was all too true. What beat snow-frocked trees, twinkling lights, soft music, and a crackling fire?

"I'm going to have to talk to your cousin about hiding those books from you."

Cora happened to know that Gabby spent a fair share of her paycheck at her cousin Isabella Clark's bookshop.

Gabby gave her a cheeky smile. "There's always the library."

The bell behind them jingled and Cora turned to see her sister Amelia come in through the door, shivering from the cold and staring longingly at the hot mugs in their hands.

"Oh!" Gabby set down her mug and held up a finger. "I have your arrangements in the back. Let me grab them."

Firefly Café, like every other establishment in town, went all out with holiday decorations. In fact, most store owners were Cora's best customers.

Gabby disappeared through the back door, leaving Cora and Amelia alone. Cora braced herself for another probing conversation, even though she usually didn't have to worry about Amelia with things like that. Amelia was more sensitive, and more private, and like her, she was less keen to meddle in other people's business.

But today she was looking at her a little nervously.

"I've been meaning to call you," she said slowly. "You won't mind if I celebrate Christmas Eve with Matt this year?"

Cora tried to hide her shock, even though she knew that she probably should have seen this coming. Since Matt Bradford had returned to town over the summer, he and Amelia had picked up right where they'd left off in high school. They'd want to celebrate Christmas together. Like Thanksgiving, the festivities would be bigger this year. Like their tree decorating night, it would be different.

"Of course." She tried to smile but her mouth felt dry. "The more the merrier."

Amelia swallowed heavily. "Actually, I meant, with the Bradfords. It's a tradition in their family to open their gifts on Christmas Eve, and well, since I'm already going to be spending Christmas Day with you guys, I…"

Cora realized that Amelia wasn't asking her for permission, but that she was merely informing her of her plans. Did Cora mind? Of course she minded! What about the fire crackling in the hearth and the overflowing bowls of popcorn, and the flannel printed pajamas, and their annual movie? They watched the same movie, every Christmas Eve, and only on Christmas Eve. She withheld every other viewing every night of December until the twenty-fourth. Didn't her sister look forward to it? What about one last night to admire the glow of the lights on the tree, and the anticipation of a morning of fun, family, and presents, even if they were too old to believe that Santa was coming?

Didn't Amelia care about any of these traditions? Didn't they mean anything to her?

And wait, she had just said the Bradfords, not Matt. Matt's parents lived in Minnesota. Surely she didn't mean Robbie's parents, because that would mean…

Her mouth went dry. "Does this mean Britt will be skipping out on our traditions too?"

Amelia frowned. "You're mad."

So it was true, of course. Robbie and Matt were cousins. Their family would have plans of their own.

"It's Britt's first Christmas back in town in years," Cora said. "I thought…"

She didn't bother to finish that. Amelia knew what Cora thought. That everything would be as it always was since they were little.

Only they weren't little anymore.

And their mother wasn't here either.

She shook her head and braved a smile, trying to pull herself together. "Sounds nice," she said simply because really, it did sound nice. But it also sounded foreign and unfamiliar. "Guess that means extra hot cocoa for me."

Shoot. Her voice hitched, and tears threatened to fall.

Amelia set a hand on her arm. "Don't be mad, Cora. We'll still be there on Christmas."

We. Meaning Amelia and Matt. Not just Amelia and Britt.

Cora's smile felt tight when she glanced her sister's way. "It's fine. Really. It makes sense for you to spend Christmas Eve with the Bradfords."

She took another sip of her coffee, finding that she'd lost the taste for it. It would be fine, she told herself. It would have to be.

And at least she still had Maddie to count on.

*

Cora was grateful that she had so many customers keeping her mind busy that afternoon. The holiday rush was in full swing, especially now that the town square was lit up with an enormous pine. With it being a short holiday season, most people in town were eager to make the most of the time, and sometimes Cora had noticed that this made them decorate more and therefore buy more than they did on the years that there was a bigger stretch between Thanksgiving and Christmas.

While personally, Cora was always disappointed in a shorter season, she couldn't deny that it strangely helped her sales, and she would need that boost to carry her through the slow winter months because try as she might, people just weren't as interested in Valentine's Day or Easter decorations, confirming her belief that Christmas was special.

"Big plans for tonight?" Natalie asked once the customers had slowed to just a few browsers.

Huge plans by Cora's standards, but she wasn't quite ready to share anything just yet. Phil might be in town for the holidays, but after that, he'd be returning to his life in the city. It was best not to get her hopes up too high.

Still, by the time she closed up for the day, she was almost too tired to be nervous at the prospect of spending an evening with Phil, but as she walked down the street toward the familiar road where the Keaton house sat, right on the waterfront, like her own childhood home, she couldn't fight the ripple that tore through her stomach. Taking a deep breath, she pressed her glove-covered finger to the doorbell and then gripped the bag of decorations with both hands.

Georgie was the one to fling open the door. Cora supposed she should have expected this and she was secretly pleased because the little girl's energy was contagious and her chatter immediately put Cora at ease.

"Daddy forgot to buy lights," she announced as Cora stomped the snow off her boots onto the mat and then began sliding them off.

Phil appeared at the end of the hallway, looking guilty as charged. "I see you've already told on me," he said in a mock scolding tone.

"There appear to be no secrets with Georgie around," Cora laughed, but a strange shadow fell over Phil's expression.

His brow knitted for a moment before he recovered quickly. "Well, I'm not really sure what to do about a tree without lights."

Cora hid a knowing smile and handed over the bag. "I had a feeling you might need these."

Phil looked in the bag at the six packages of lights and laughed. "What do I owe you?"

Cora brushed his offer away. "This isn't your boardroom, sir. Here in Blue Harbor, we share. We're neighborly like that."

"Don't tell me that people also knock on each other's doors without an invitation," he said.

"Of course! And at this time of year, it's called caroling!" When he laughed, she pointed to the bag of lights. "I have more in stock than I will ever sell. One year I sold out and I promised myself never to let that happen again. Consider it an early Christmas gift."

"Well, thank you," Phil said sincerely. He set the bag down on a console table. "Here, let me take your coat."

Cora unwound her scarf and unbuttoned her coat, her heart speeding up when Phil helped her slip out of the parka. She was wearing another of her favorite sweaters—a creamy angora scoop neck with the gold necklace that she usually saved for special occasions.

Was it sad that this was such a rare occurrence in her life? That she was already twenty-nine and she couldn't even remember the last time she'd gone on a date, much less spent any amount of time with an attractive, single man?

And Phil was attractive, possibly even more so tonight, now that it was the first time she was seeing him without a coat on. His navy wool sweater revealed broad shoulders and strong arms, and in casual jeans, he seemed taller than she remembered, but then, she was no longer standing with the extra heel of her boots.

She followed him to the front room, where the dark tree sat in the corner, next to the fireplace. She immediately realized that Phil was in dire need of her help, and not just because of his oversight when it came to the lights.

"Does the fireplace work?" Cora inquired. She'd spotted a stack of firewood just outside the house, covered in a tarp. The Keatons hadn't lived here in almost a year, and while she knew the neighbors kept an eye on things here and there, she hoped that it wasn't rain-soaked.

Phil looked surprised at the suggestion and then shrugged. "Don't see why not. I'll grab some logs from outside."

While he did that, Cora quickly found an old-fashioned radio and turned the dial to her favorite station, the one that played Christmas carols twenty-four hours a day all through the season, and which of course made her sisters groan about seven days into it back when they were younger.

By the time Phil returned, with snow dusting the top of his dark, wavy hair, things were almost starting to feel festive, and Georgie was practically dancing with excitement.

Phil grinned as he closed the door behind him, shutting out the cold wind and securing them all in this warm, cozy house. Cora looked around as he crouched at the base of the hearth, albeit mostly to stop herself from staring at the way his wide shoulders strained and moved as he tended to the logs.

"This is a lovely house," Cora said. "Actually, the owners of this house also own my shop. Well, not the shop, but the building."

Phil nodded slowly and said, without turning toward her, "They're my grandparents."

"Really?" Cora took a moment to process that, along with the fact that he hadn't said so earlier when she'd referred to her landlords. "Well, small world!"

Now that she thought about it, Mrs. Keaton did mention a grandson, one that was helping to set them up in a smaller, assisted-living apartment. Her eyes shone when she spoke of him, even though she never mentioned her own son. Rumor had it that there had been a falling out years ago.

Perhaps this was the reason why Phil had been quiet about his connection to them.

Cora considered this new information. Phil's grandmother loved Christmas! She attended every festival and event in town and always bought a few items from Cora's store, too. The very last item she bought when she told Cora about the move was a gold-painted serving tray. She said she still planned to make her famous roasted chestnuts for her husband, as she did every year. Didn't her traditions get passed down to Phil and Georgie?

"Your grandmother was always so proud of you," Cora said now, and it was true. Mrs. Keaton always lit up like a Christmas tree when she spoke of her only grandchild. How he was handsome, intelligent, thoughtful, and kind. She spoke the truth, Cora thought. "How are they doing?"

"As well as can be expected," Phil said on a sigh. "But they're getting up there in age, and…I'm not sure they'll be getting back here anytime soon." His jaw seemed to clench at that, but he didn't elaborate.

Cora nodded thoughtfully. It was a shame, but so long as her rent money was directly withdrawn from her account each month, she supposed that their business relationship could withstand the distance.

Phil sucked in a long breath as he rolled back on his heels and stood. Inside the hearth, the fire crackled tentatively, and he crouched again to poke at the logs until the flames grew stronger.

"There," he said proudly. He glanced at Georgie and raised his eyebrows. "What do you think?"

"I think it's beginning to feel like Christmas!" Georgie cried.

"Can I get you a glass of wine?" Phil asked, turning his attention to Cora.

She nodded and followed him into the kitchen, which was as unchanged as the front of the house. A throwback in time, with well-worn wood floors, maple cabinets, and a baker's rack stuffed with cookbooks, much like the one in the kitchen of her own childhood home.

"So you used to visit then?"

Phil nodded. "Once a year or so, mostly on my own because my parents were busy. My dad had his own law firm. It wasn't easy to get away."

"Not even at Christmas?" she asked.

He glanced at her. "Especially at Christmas."

He opened a few drawers before finding a corkscrew. Cora couldn't help but realize he might have bought the wine just because of her visit, but then she banished that hope immediately. Nonsense. It was a Saturday night. He worked all day, from what she gathered. It was probably just his first occasion to have any since he arrived.

But when he pulled the bottle from the shelf, she noted the label with a smile. "Conway?" Now she realized with a flutter that he *had* bought it just for her.

He gave a little smile. "It didn't seem right to buy anything else, and I couldn't help noticing that the grocery store gives your family's wine prominent display."

Cora laughed as she accepted the glass. It was one of her favorite blends.

"I actually think I remember going to the orchard once on one of my visits," he said, squinting as if at a memory. "It was summer, and there was some event with cherries."

"The Cherry Festival!" Cora grinned, pleased that he would have known it and curious if she'd ever seen him there, but never noticed, being a kid at the time. "One of our family's favorite events of the year."

"Your family likes its traditions," he said. He occupied himself twisting the cork, frowning slightly.

Cora fell silent for a moment. It would seem that the same wasn't to be said for the Keatons. "Well, you'll have to take Georgie sometime once the weather warms up," Cora said, and then, realizing that she wasn't so sure she wanted to hear about Phil's long-term plans, she took a long sip of the wine, letting it warm her throat.

"This is actually the first time that Georgie's ever been to Blue Harbor," Phil said. He gave a little smile. "Between my job, and then Georgie going to live with her mother, the occasion never came along before now, I'm afraid. At least it's been a success so far."

"So you'll admit to enjoying this small-town Christmas?"

His grin was rueful. "It's made Georgie happy, and…that's what Christmas is about, right? Kids and presents and all that?"

Cora gaped at him. He couldn't be serious. "Christmas is about family and hope and creating memories that should last a lifetime!"

He stared at her, and her cheeks felt warm. She'd gone too far, acted "Christmas crazy" as her sisters used to joke, even though she knew they were only teasing.

"With my mother gone, sometimes those memories are all I have," she explained.

Phil's gaze was steady on hers, and she looked away, eager to change the subject. "But Georgie is definitely happy, that much is true."

Hearing her name, Georgie called out, "Are you guys coming in? I need help with the lights!"

Cora exchanged a look with Phil. "Guess that's our cue."

They walked back into the living room, where already Georgie was starting to tear into the ornaments that Phil had bought from the store.

"Now, here's a trick," Cora said. "You have to start with the lights first."

"I'll do the honors," Phil said gamely, and Cora sat back, not even twitching when they were clustered on some branches and sparse on others. The joy in Georgie's eyes confirmed that the lights didn't need to be perfect; they were perfect for her.

And wasn't that what made Christmas traditions so wonderful? Each family had its own way of doing things.

Or at least her family did. Once.

Phil looked over to her, giving her a quizzical expression. "Everything okay? I mean, the lights aren't as perfect as the trees in your store, but…"

Cora laughed. "The lights are perfect. It's silly, really. My two older sisters made other plans for Christmas Eve and, well…it's disappointing."

To say the least. She'd been fighting back a pull in her chest all day, considered going so far as to just watch their beloved holiday movie on her own, tonight, maybe.

But then she remembered that Maddie would be counting on her, much the way they had all once counted on her to uphold their traditions.

"I'm starting to get the impression that Christmas is a big thing in your family." Phil handed her an ornament, and Cora searched for just the right branch to hang it from.

She laughed. "Gee, I wonder what gave that away. But, yes, my mother loved Christmas. It was her favorite time of the year and she always made it beautiful and special. When she was gone, it was important for me to keep her traditions going. It made me feel like she was still with us in a way. Harbor Holidays allows me to do just that."

Phil frowned deeply and then cleared his throat.

Cora didn't want to dwell. It made her sad, when Christmas was supposed to be a time of joy. "What about your family?" She hoped she hadn't overstepped.

It was pretty obvious that Phil was a divorced, single dad, who didn't make much of the holiday on his own, but she was curious about the Keatons, and what exactly had transpired that led to Phil coming back to town, alone, with Georgie. Why suddenly introduce her to Blue Harbor if his grandparents were now living somewhere else and closer to where he lived?

"Not unless you call eating at one of the most expensive hotels in the city as a big deal," Phil said. He shrugged. "My parents liked to get out on to the town, go to parties, get dressed up. See and be seen, you might say."

"And you?"

"Me?" He jutted his lip as if he hadn't considered it. "I always got what I wanted for Christmas. No complaints here." He grinned, but his eyes fell flat.

Cora frowned at this, knowing that she would be miserable spending her holidays that way, thinking that Mrs. Keaton would be too.

"I guess the thing I like most about this time of year is that everyone is home."

She was sure at least one of her sisters would have shot her a look for admitting to this. Sure, she was a homebody, everyone knew that, but wasn't that what made Christmas so special? It wasn't just about the lights and the gifts and the food. It was about the simple joy of being home, surrounded by those you loved the most.

Or, in this year's case, maybe not.

They finished decorating the tree and then sat on the couch to admire it, Georgie sipping her hot chocolate, and Cora and Phil drinking their wine.

"I bet this tree is just as pretty as your tree, Cora," Georgie said.

Cora sputtered on her wine. "Actually, I have a confession. I don't have a tree of my own."

Phil pulled back against a throw pillow, looking at her in mock horror. "But Christmas is just around the corner!"

"You have to hurry before they're all gone!" Georgie insisted.

Cora knew she had this coming. "Actually, I never get a tree of my own. I figure I have the trees downstairs and the one at my family's house. That always felt like my tree."

Until Candy took charge of decorating it, she thought.

"Maybe it's a good idea to have a tree of your own. Something separate from your shop?" Phil pointed out.

She winced. "I guess I don't see the point…"

"Wait a minute." Phil shifted on the couch until he was leaning toward her, his look stern. "You two gave me a hard time about not having a tree."

"But you have Georgie," Cora laughed. "I guess I feel like a tree is something to decorate together. A tradition worth sharing."

Phil met her gaze, all amusement gone from his eyes as their gazes locked. Cora felt her breath catch, and for a moment, even the sounds of the carols couldn't compete with the beating of her heart.

"I couldn't agree more," he said softly.

Cora pulled in a sigh and took a sip of wine to fight the flutter in her stomach. The embers in the fireplace were dying down and Cora didn't need to look at the clock to know that it was getting late. Georgie's yawns were telling enough.

"Well, I should probably get going," she said, setting her wine glass on an end table.

"I hope the roads have been cleared," Phil said.

"Oh, I walked," Cora replied.

"Walked? In this temperature?" Phil looked downright horrified.

"I'm sure you do a lot of walking in the city," she pointed out.

"Well, yes," Phil admitted, frowning. "But in the city, everything is lit up."

Cora gave a little smile. "I have the light of the moon. And when it reflects off the snow, it's more than bright enough. Besides, I love walking in the snow at this time of year. It feels…magical." She took her coat from the rack and shrugged into it.

"I have a feeling that I'm not going to talk you into letting me drive you home." Phil raised an eyebrow.

"You're not," Cora said. She jutted her chin to the living room. "Besides, it looks like someone is almost asleep. She'll need to save some energy for all that gingerbread decorating tomorrow."

"I have a feeling that Georgie is going to insist on going." Phil glanced over his shoulder where Georgie was now curling up with a blanket on the couch, clearly worn out from the excitement of the day.

"Oh, she can't miss it," Cora said firmly. "Much too special."

"Good night then," he said, seeming to hesitate.

Cora felt her stomach flutter as she reached for the doorknob. She could have stayed all night, and maybe he wanted her to. But it was time to go. For now.

*

Phil watched out the window as Cora disappeared into the nightfall. He would have felt a lot better if she'd let him drive her home, and he still had half a mind to tuck Georgie into the backseat of his car and do just that.

Ironic, he supposed, that he was so determined to protect the one woman he was about to hurt.

Grimacing against the bitterness that formed in his mouth, he walked back into the kitchen and rinsed the wine glasses, washing away the reminder of the nicest evening he'd spent in a while, and not just because it had been a long time since he'd seen Georgie so happy. Cora was a breath of fresh air—not like any of the other women that he'd dated since his divorce. She didn't seem to care what kind of car he drove or how fat his bank account was or where they might have dinner. She cared about…traditions, he thought, as he circled back into the living room and admired the fully decorated tree.

It was just like the one his grandmother put up that one Christmas he'd spent here—well, minus the pink ornaments. Still, it stood in the same corner of the living room, lighting up the space with the same feeling of wonder he'd felt all those years ago when he was the same age as Georgie was now. They'd baked cookies, and decorated, and his grandfather had even pulled his old guitar out of the attic and attempted a few carols. It wasn't the fanciest Christmas he'd ever had, but it was definitely the most special.

And it was the only one.

This could be a special Christmas for Georgie, though. One last memory to hold onto—of this house, of the one time in his childhood when the world felt full of something other than things. Christmas in Blue Harbor, with Georgie, and carols, and a fire crackling in the hearth.

He hadn't thought of it until now. Hadn't wanted to, really.

And now, it was too late.

Next year Georgie would be spending the holidays with her mother.

And this house would be sold to a new family. And he'd have no reason to come back here at all.

Even though it might just be the only place he'd ever been happy. Then. And now.

7

Cora woke earlier than her alarm the next morning, happy to see through her parted curtains that there was a fresh dusting of snow on the tree branches outside her window.

She strained her ear, wondering where the sound that had woken her was coming from. It was a banging sound and not one that was typically heard at this hour on Main Street in Blue Harbor. The town was usually quiet, muffled by the fresh snow and the knowledge that most people were tucked in their warm beds.

She tossed her legs over the side of the bed, wedged her feet into her oversized and extra soft Santa slippers (a gift from Maddie last year), and put on her Mrs. Clause robe (a top seller downstairs at the store).

The sound was coming from the back door, and only those who knew her well would know that this was her primary entrance to her personal living space. Others might assume that she came and went through the shop door, though considering it was nearly as much her home as this small apartment, she couldn't exactly say they were wrong.

It was probably one of her sisters—Britt most likely, considering that Amelia and Maddie both went into their kitchens early to get a start on the day. Britt, perhaps, coming to apologize in person for bailing on Christmas Eve.

Cora opened the door to see Bart standing outside, gripping a medium-sized fir tree by the trunk. He gave her the once-over, from her robe to her slippers, doing a poor job of hiding his smile.

"You really do love Christmas," he marveled, chuckling under his breath.

"Obviously!" she replied, not feeling embarrassed at her attire. This was Bart. Friend Bart. Still, she was almost thankful that it wasn't Phil. He probably wouldn't be quite as understanding that she was dressed like she had just come from the North Pole. "And you don't?"

"Not eleven months of the year," Bart said. "But something tells me that you do, and it's not just an act."

Cora jutted her chin defiantly. "I love Christmas every day of the year. In fact, if it wouldn't take away from the magic of the holiday, I would celebrate Christmas year-round."

"Then why is this my first time ever delivering a tree to your door?" Bart arched an eyebrow.

Cora frowned at him, not bothering to point out that she hardly needed a tree of her own when she had an entire inventory of them right here in her shop. There was a bigger topic here to discuss.

"I didn't order a tree."

"No, but someone ordered one for you. Left a message last night for this to be delivered first thing this morning." He looked over her shoulder into her kitchen, which was obviously decorated with snowman cookie jars, a red tea kettle, festive dish towels, and of course, red placemats on her pedestal table. "Where do you want it?"

Cora shook her head. "Wait. Someone ordered this for me?"

Bart nodded. "That's right."

"Well, who was it?" Cora asked impatiently.

Bart just shrugged. "Didn't say."

Cora blinked. Who would do this? She didn't know why she even bothered with the next question but decided that she may as well narrow down the list of potential suspects anyway. Chances were high it was one of her sisters, cousins, or…Candy.

"Was it a man or a woman?"

"I don't know. They left a message through my online order form. I rarely get one of those come through except for some of the businesses in town."

"Well, they must have left a name!" Cora said impatiently. Really, everyone knew everyone else in Blue Harbor. Of course Bart knew who sent it.

"Look, I'm just the delivery man, and I get the impression that if they wanted their identity revealed they would tell you. Are you part of some Secret Santa program?"

"No," Cora said, but then she tucked that piece of information away for another time. Maybe next year she would start a Secret Santa campaign—it could drive business to the store.

"The invoice came through as paid, so I didn't dig deeper. You want me to check the name?"

Cora hesitated and then shook her head. "I suppose you're right. If they wanted to reveal themselves to me, they would on their own. It might be better this way."

"My thoughts exactly. Now, do you want the tree or not? In case you didn't notice, it's about ten degrees out here."

Cora opened the door wider to let him in and led him up the back stairs, her lips pursing at the way he laughed heartily at her Christmas-themed kitchen.

"Look, I end up keeping all the stuff that doesn't sell," she replied in her defense.

Bart gave her a long look over his shoulder when he reached the top floor, balancing the tree on the landing. "I almost believe that. So why don't you have a tree? Now that I'm here, I'm actually curious."

"I'm surrounded by trees all day," Cora replied, as she padded down the hall to her living room. She pushed aside an armchair to make space for the tree in the corner near the great big window that overlooked Main Street in all its wintery glory. "I mean, do you have a tree?"

He cut her a look. "Yeah. I have a tree. Of course, I do."

Oh. Cora sniffed and backed away as Bart began expertly setting it up. She had to admit that it looked huge and beautiful and festive among the other decorations that, like the items in her kitchen, were mostly leftover from the shop.

"So you really don't know who called about it?" she asked. Maybe she should ask him to check the order form, just so she could stop wondering and get on with her day.

"Maybe it's a secret admirer," Bart teased.

"Or maybe it's my sister feeling guilty because she bailed on our Christmas Eve traditions." Amelia had clearly felt bad about breaking the news to her. It would be just like Amelia to try to do something to cheer her up or smooth over the disappointment.

Bart shrugged. "Anyway, enjoy it. I should probably get down to the lot before someone comes along and swipes a tree."

Cora considered this. There was never any crime in Blue Harbor, other than some occasional misdemeanors with teenagers or over-served tourists in the summer. "Has that ever happened?"

He laughed. "There's a first for everything, right?"

Cora turned back to look at her great, big, beautiful tree that was all hers, in her home, and nodded. Yes, there really was a first for everything.

Even a new tradition.

*

A few hours later, after sending Natalie home to pick up her daughter from the sitter, Cora handled the last few customers of what would be a short work day and turned the sign on the door. Yes, she was closing early, but there was little point in staying open when the entire town would soon be heading over to the town hall for the gingerbread event.

And a few out-of-towners would hopefully show up, too, Cora thought.

She arrived ten minutes before the doors officially opened, telling herself that it wasn't because she was excited at the prospect of seeing Phil and Georgie again, but because she wanted to have a chance to thank Amelia properly for gifting her the tree before the day turned too chaotic. The more Cora considered the sender, the more she was certain it was her sweet-natured sister. (While Candy wasn't shy about grand gestures, she would never be able to resist wanting credit.)

But when she arrived at the town hall, Amelia was frantically setting up the various stations, assisted by Maddie and, of course, Candy.

"Oh, another helper!" Candy cried out as soon as she spotted Cora across the room.

Amelia and Maddie both looked relieved, though Cora couldn't be sure if it was because she had two extra hands or because she might be able to provide a buffer with their father's girlfriend. Cora refrained from pointing out to Amelia that she never had to hire her to work at the café, but then, Candy was quite helpful and eager to please.

Candy smiled at her and held up her flour-coated hands. "I'd hug you but I wouldn't want to get you all messy."

Saved! Not that there was anything wrong with a hug. It was just that lately, the person Cora wanted to be hugging her was...Phil. She could still feel his arms when he caught her on Thanksgiving, and she wasn't about to admit how many times she'd replayed that day in her mind ever since.

"That's okay, Candy. I understand," Cora said politely. She glanced at Amelia, who gave her a pointed look, and then turned away, hiding her smile.

While she went to the hallway where coat racks were set up, she took in the scene. It was the same event, every year, she knew, but this year she could see it had her sisters' marks on it. As coordinators of the event this year, and typical to the personalities of all the Conway family members, they had embraced the challenge. The rows of decorating tables were covered in red and white striped tablecloths, and the topping options were more than just crushed candy canes and sprinkles. She spotted everything from gumdrops to ribbon candy to mini marshmallows in passing. And then there were the gingerbread baking stations, each with measuring spoons and cups, and canisters of flour and sugar. But the best new additions were the large recipe signs that had been written onto the chalkboards all around the room. Attached to the bottom of each was a tear-away sheet.

"This is clever," Cora commented, recalling Gladys O'Leary's rather unimaginative effort last year when she'd simply dumped a grocery bag at each station and called it a day. But then, after twenty years, she was probably ready to pass the torch.

Cora hoped that her sisters would make the tradition last just as long.

"I like that it gives people a chance to gather together and mingle," Candy said, coming to stand next to her.

Cora could only hope that Candy had washed her hands when she put an arm around her shoulder and gave it a good, hard squeeze. Just in case there was any hope of Phil stopping by, she'd worn her best cashmere sweater, telling herself that a community event was a reason to dress up a bit, anyway.

She glanced at her sisters, who were dressed festively, but practically. If they got flour or icing on their jeans or sweaters, it would wash right out.

Luckily, Candy didn't seem to be onto anything amiss. Yet.

"And look," Candy was saying, sweeping her hand over the room, like a game show host. "We have hot chocolate at the concessions stand. I'm in charge." She waggled her eyebrows, and Cora had to bite her lip to keep from laughing.

She should have known that her sisters would have found a creative way to keep Candy occupied without getting too meddlesome. And this solution was perfect. Candy loved to help. And she loved to chat with everyone.

And decorate, Cora thought, considering the garish tinsel that now framed the concession window, complete by flashing lights and a cardboard sign that read, "Candy Cane Hot Chocolate."

Candy tapped her apron, which bore the print of a large candy cane, suitable for the event, though Cora had to assume there was more to it than that.

She was right.

"That's me. Candy cane. Just through the season." Candy laughed until she snorted and gave Cora a heavy swat on the arm to underscore her joke.

Cora forced her mouth into a smile. She reminded herself that Candy meant well, but given Candy's love of themes, she was beginning to dread what the woman might have planned for their Christmas Eve dinner, now that Amelia would no longer be participating.

Usually, Amelia cooked a delicious meal, and they all gathered around the table before settling in for their movie and popcorn. Now she wondered what they would eat. Tomato and mozzarella ball kabobs shaped like a cane? She could see it now.

Speaking of Amelia…She was currently walking toward the industrial kitchen, and now might just be Cora's chance to get her alone.

Candy, however, had other ideas. "I saw you walking around the tree lighting ceremony with that single father. Quite dashing, isn't he?"

Her eyes were wide with curiosity, and Cora suppressed a sigh. She should have known she wouldn't be left off the hook so easily.

"He's very nice. And it's good to see tourist activity this time of year!" Anything to throw Candy off the scent. She took credit for matching up Maddie and Cole, and she also felt she played a fair part in reuniting Amelia and Matt. Cora was now the only single sister.

Why couldn't Candy move on to the other Conway girls? Uncle Steve's daughters? Or Aunt Miriam's nieces? Cora knew full well how much Natalie was hoping to find love…which was why it was probably a good thing that she hadn't been in the shop the few times that Phil came through.

Cora gave an apologetic glance to Candy. "I'm just going to grab Amelia before things get too busy."

"Better be quick," Candy noted with a gesture toward the doors. "People come early to get a good station."

That they did. No one wanted to be stuck too close to the front doors, where a draft could blow in from the stairwell, or too far from the kitchen, where the ovens needed to be watched. But Cora couldn't think about claiming a prime spot just now. She hurried across the floor toward the kitchen, nearly out of breath by the time she found Amelia near the sink, washing her hands.

"I just wanted to say thank you," she said. When Amelia gave her a quizzical look, she added, "For the tree. I knew it had to be from you—"

But Amelia was shaking her head. "Tree?"

"You didn't send me a Christmas tree?" Cora picked up a bowl of dough along with Amelia and followed her to the door. "I guess I assumed because of Christmas Eve…" She trailed off when she saw the dismay in her sister's eyes.

"I'm really sorry, Cora. And Britt is, too. I'm sure she'll want to talk to you today. The holidays are special, but they can't be the same every year, can they? It's fun to try new things and have some new celebrations." She gave her a smile of encouragement.

Cora didn't want to get into that conversation just now, not with the event about to start. Not with her feelings still sore. "So, you didn't send the tree?"

"I'm sorry, Cora, but I have no idea what you're talking about. I didn't send you a Christmas tree. Now I sort of wish I had, though." She gave her an apologetic smile.

Cora made a mental list of all of her family members, wondering who might have sent one and why now of all years. Her cousins cared, but not enough to be bothered pushing something on her that she hadn't asked for, and Britt and Maddie were too busy with their new business ventures these past few months to take on much more.

"But if it wasn't you, then who was it?"

Amelia shrugged and flashed Cora a smile. "Sounds like you have a secret admirer."

A secret admirer. Wouldn't that be nice?

"This has Candy written all over it," Cora sighed, thinking again of the tension the other night over the tree topper. "Maybe it's her way of letting me know it's time to have my own tree to decorate."

"You could ask her," Amelia said, as she set the bowl down on a table that was quickly descended upon by Keira and a friend. "But isn't it fun to think that it could be from someone else?"

Cora thought about Candy and shook her head. As much as she could dream of something as romantic as a secret admirer, she lived in Blue Harbor, where everyone knew everyone, and the only eligible suitor in town was leaving in a matter of weeks.

Candy didn't like tension. She would want to smooth things over for the night.

It was sweet. A relief in many ways because now Cora might not need to worry too much about Candy overstepping any more traditions—not if she felt repentant.

"Oh, Cora, good, there you are!" Maddie came over to her with flushed cheeks and bright eyes. Her dark auburn hair was pulled back off her face, but a few wisps had come undone.

"Do you need some help?" Cora was happy to tend to any last-minute decorations.

Maddie's expression looked pained, and she didn't need to say anything for Cora to know what was coming.

"Don't tell me," she groaned.

"Don't be mad!" Maddie blinked rapidly. "It's just that Cole doesn't have any family, and our family is…well, a lot. And we did Thanksgiving at the house, and we'll be there Christmas Day. I just thought that if Amelia and Britt weren't going to be there, that the whole thing would sort of be… canceled." Maddie winced.

Cora gaped at her sister. "Cancelled? And what about me?"

"You're upset."

Clearly! Cora thought back on Amelia's words as she pushed back the disappointment that tugged at her chest. "No, you're right. We'll have Christmas. And it makes sense for you to do something special with Cole on Christmas Eve."

Maddie reached in and gave Cora a quick squeeze before dashing off. "I knew you'd understand!"

Yes, Cora understood, all right. Her sisters were moving on with their lives. They were starting new traditions of their own.

She blinked back tears and took a steadying breath, just in time to see Phil and Georgie arrive in the doorway across the hall.

And so could she.

Maybe Amelia was right, Cora thought. She was trying some new things this season, with a new person. And it *was* fun.

*

Phil stared down at the gingerbread dough and tried not to think of all the work he still had to do before tomorrow's weekly Monday meeting, never mind the fact that he still hadn't given Cora notice on the shop.

It was what she had said, last night, about her mother, and Christmas, and traditions. It got to him, damn it. And nothing ever got to him when it came to business. And that's all this was. A simple transaction. He was the executor of his grandparents' estate. He was here to do what was in their best interest, and that was to cash out their properties, give them a much-needed nest egg. They had no reason to hold onto the cottage or the house on Main. That part of their life was behind them now.

And behind him too, he reminded himself. Coming back here had muddled with his head. Stirred up memories that he hadn't thought of in years, evoking a time and a feeling that were fleeting, not part of daily life. At least, not his.

But they could be Georgie's. At least for the holidays.

"Here comes my sister Britt," Cora said, barely looking up from the workstation, and something in her tone told Phil that it wasn't because she was a perfectionist when it came to rolling out gingerbread.

Sure enough, the woman from the cider stand arrived with a girl around Georgie's age. "Hey, Cora. Hi, Phil. Georgie. This is Keira Bradford. She was hoping that Georgie might help her decorate some gingerbread men at the children's table."

Georgie smiled up at him. "Can I, Dad?"

"Of course!" He pulled in a breath as he watched the two girls scamper off together. Soon he'd be alone with Cora. What was his excuse now?

Technically, he didn't have a buyer for either of the properties—yet. But giving ample notice was not only the professional but kind thing to do. Meaning the sooner he got it over with, the better.

But now Cora was rolling out her dough with increased force, and her sister was frowning. Deeply.

"Amelia told me that she talked to you," she said.

Phil had the impression that he was about to get involved in a family spat, not that he was immune from them. The holidays tended to bring out the worst in people, at least in his experience.

"Maddie did too," Cora said archly. She sighed and set down the rolling pin. Phil couldn't help but notice that Britt looked a little relieved about that. "It's okay. I understand."

"You sure?" Britt chewed her bottom lip.

"I'm sure." Beside him, he saw Cora wink, and something in Britt transform.

"Well, then, I should get back to Robbie before he finishes frosting all the roofs. It was always my favorite part," she added. "I forgot how much I missed this event. I guess I forgot how much I missed a lot of things in Blue Harbor."

"It's certainly a special place."

Phil stiffened and focused on his task. Cora's words had touched a nerve, even though they weren't directed at him.

"Everything okay with your sister?" Phil asked when they were alone again. Cora was standing so close to him that he could feel the sleeve of her sweater brush his arm every once and a while. He inched closer, liking the sensation.

"Oh, she bailed on Christmas Eve, too." Cora shrugged. "And Maddie did earlier."

"So your special traditions?"

"Guess they forced my hand. I'll have to make some new ones this year." She gave him a long look before glancing away. "We should probably get these in the oven before the dough gets too warm and they lose their shape. Our first batch should be just about done by now, too."

They walked to the kitchen, past the children's table to check on Georgie, who was giggling as she placed gumdrop buttons on a gingerbread man.

"She seems to be fitting right in," Cora observed.

Yes, Phil thought. She was. But then, Blue Harbor was like that. Then, and now. It was the leaving that was hardest. The reminder that life wasn't always like this.

"It's nice to see her with other kids. As an only child, I worry that she'll be lonely."

Cora glanced up at him before pushing through the kitchen door. "Were you lonely as an only child?"

"How'd you—" He stopped. "Of course. My grandmother told you."

"I knew that you were an only child, just like your father. She said the two of you were a lot alike."

Phil felt his jaw tighten. He'd spent his entire life trying to earn his father's approval and hadn't ever felt like he measured up. But now, thinking maybe they were a lot alike no longer felt like a compliment.

They managed to get to one of the ovens just as another woman was pulling a tray out. Cora set the timer and checked on their earlier batch.

"A few more minutes," the woman remarked. She glanced at the two of them and gave Cora a little smile. "I'll be popping into your shop this week. Still need to pick up some stocking stuffers for the grandkids."

"I'll be there!" Cora said happily.

Oh, good grief. Phil couldn't talk to her about all this now. Not with what she'd just said. Not with all these people here. This was her community. Where everyone knew everyone.

And where everyone probably knew his grandparents, too.

Besides, as he watched Cora open the oven door and slide in the tray, his gaze drifted to her curves, and he felt something stronger than the desire to close a business deal, which usually gave him a rush, every time. He felt something more like attraction. A yearning for something deeper, and different.

Something that was right in front of him. Cora blinked up at him, her eyes questioning, until suddenly her expression fell.

"Oh dear God," Cora hissed under her breath. "Hurry up and get into the pantry. Candy's coming."

"But isn't our timer about to go off?" Phil wasn't much of a baker, but he knew plenty about burning food. Georgie would no doubt be sharing stories of his overcooked pizzas before long.

"They'll be fine, and something tells me that we won't be if Candy finds out we've partnered up."

"She's determined to match you up, isn't she?" Phil said as he let her gently push him into a broom closet.

Cora kept the door open a crack so she could peer through it. "Pretty much. She'll try anyone so long as they're male, single, and employed."

"Guess I fit the bill then," Phil said, trying not to laugh.

Cora looked genuinely apologetic as she turned to look up at him. "No, I didn't mean it like that. I mean, obviously, Candy took one look at you and made a point of finding out your situation."

"My situation?" It wasn't so easy to suppress the grin that was pulling at his mouth.

Cora's eyes widened and then shifted to the side. Her cheeks flamed. "I mean, you know, if you were single, and, um…"

He lifted an eyebrow and offered, "Employed?"

"Right." Cora swallowed hard. "And of course of the right age…"

"Bare basics, then. No other real criteria needed. Just a plain and simple match. No…physical requirements?"

She narrowed her eyes. "Are you fishing for a compliment?"

Now he grinned. "No. Just seeing where I fit into all of this."

Cora huffed and pursed her lips. "Obviously Candy saw something in you."

"Only Candy?"

Their eyes locked. In this room, they were so close that Phil could smell the perfume she was wearing, although he wasn't so sure it was perfume. It was sweet, and spicy, with a bit of pine mixed in there too. She smelled like Christmas, he realized.

She smelled like the way he wanted to feel. Then. Now. Always.

His gaze lingered on her mouth and he heard Cora pull in a breath before just as quickly the door was yanked open and Candy's face appeared.

"Well, what do we have here?" She looked just as elated at finding them as Cora did embarrassed.

"We just needed a broom. Um…Georgie spilled something." Cora shot him a panicked look and mouthed, "Sorry."

"And here I thought there was a sprig of mistletoe hiding out somewhere!" Candy peered up at the ceiling and then gave Phil a coy wink as she strutted away.

"Don't mind her," Cora said, but from the pink in her cheeks, it was clear that she minded Candy, very much. "We should probably check on the gingerbread anyway."

Phil supposed she was right. Now wasn't the time for a kiss. Or a conversation about the property. Both those things would have to wait.

Maybe, only one of them could, he thought. The more he got to know Cora, the more he doubted she would ever speak to him again if he booted her from the storefront.

A beeping sound was coming from the oven as they approached, and the smell made it clear that it had been going on for quite some time.

"Damn," Cora said, dropping the tray of burnt gingerbread onto the counter.

"No one will notice if we cover them in icing. And it's still the best gingerbread I ever made," Phil said, trying to cajole her.

She narrowed her eyes on him. "More like the *only* gingerbread you ever made?"

He laughed. "Well, I did make cookies before. Once. But I was more of an assistant. My grandmother was the baker."

Cora gave him a soft smile. "Well, we can call this a practice run, and I'm sure your grandmother would be proud."

He swallowed hard, considering those words. Proud? He'd never thought to make his grandparents proud; he'd been too busy trying to impress his father. But now he thought about everything he'd done and was doing. He wasn't so sure how his grandmother would feel about him at all if she knew that he was planning to sell her properties in Blue Harbor.

"Besides," Cora said with a mischievous gleam in her eye. "It was worth it to see Candy's expression when she opened the door on us."

It would have been an even more amusing expression if she'd caught them kissing, which she might have done if she'd held off a few more seconds.

Phil didn't know what to make of that. He should be relieved, really, that they'd been interrupted before he went and did something that made all of this even more complicated than it already was.

But now, looking into her pretty blue eyes, he felt the pull again, to go with something he hadn't factored into his life in a long time. His heart.

He was leaning in, he realized, letting something other than common sense guide him. Cora was looking up at him, her gaze searching, and before he could do something he regretted, he reached up a hand and lightly brushed some flour from her cheek with the pad of his thumb. Her skin was soft, smooth, and warm.

"Flour," he said, holding up the evidence.

"Oh." Cora blinked and then brushed a hand to her face, scrubbing at the remnants.

"I should probably check on Georgie," he said, eager to get out of the kitchen. It was better once they were in the big room, surrounded by people huddled at tables, all talking, laughing, while carols blasted from the speakers. He could almost picture his grandmother at one of the tables, happily rolling out dough or lining up gumdrops. These were her friends. Her community.

And he was about to take away her last ties to it, even though he knew that there was no sense in holding onto it.

That there never had been, or so he'd once believed.

"She's having a great time," Cora observed, watching the little girls with a smile.

Phil looked down at her, admiring the way her eyes glimmered from such a simple pleasure. One that he, too, was enjoying.

"I am too," he admitted.

Cora looked at him, her grin turning teasing. "See? I knew there was some Christmas spirit in you, after all."

Phil shook his head as he walked back into the crowded room to find his daughter.

His Christmas spirit had been buried in a deep place a long, long time ago. Leave it to Cora of all people to dig it out of him.

8

The snow fell for days, and even though it was steady, Cora kept an eye on the windows of the shop, hoping that it would stick and that they would have a white Christmas.

In truth, she was hoping for something else, too. A visit from Phil. A run-in at the bakery or café. Something that would make her stop thinking about that moment at the gingerbread event and if it had all been in her head. That more had come from it than a lopsided cookie house with a candy-covered roof.

Her hope panned out on Wednesday afternoon, when she saw Phil and Georgie coming down Main Street on her way back from delivering a holiday wreath to Bella Clark at the bookstore. They were up ahead, coming toward her, the oversized pom-pom on Georgie's red hat flopping adorably.

She slowed her pace so that she wouldn't reach her shop before she had a chance to say hello, but there was no need. Georgie had spotted her and broke away from Phil, running toward her excitedly. "It's the Christmas lady!"

Cora laughed, especially at Phil's frown.

"Her name is Cora, Georgie," he corrected.

"I know, but she's also the Christmas lady!" Georgie insisted, and Phil just shook his head, giving her a look of apology.

"I'm flattered," she told him, once they were standing closer. His eyes were clear and lit with amusement, and his grin sent a chill down her that had nothing to do with the wind. "And it's true! I am the Christmas lady!" She hesitated, knowing that it was cold and that she should probably get back inside, but it was a slow day, and the winter weather didn't bother her much, and not just because she was dressed in a warm coat and scarf, either. Seeing Phil again, well, it was pretty hard to think about anything else.

"What are you up to today?" she asked, wondering if Georgie had roped Phil into more festivities. Ice skating at the town square, perhaps? Or maybe picking up some more decorations for the house?

"Daddy has a meeting." Georgie crossed her arms and pouted dramatically. "He always has meetings."

Phil held up his hands. "Business doesn't stop just because it's Christmas."

Cora knew this much was true, but she had the sense that Phil rarely stopped working, and that Christmas wasn't exactly high on his radar. Still, he was trying to give Georgie a good holiday, and she knew firsthand growing up how much her father struggled as a single parent at times.

"Just a short meeting this time," he told Georgie. He drew a breath, raising his eyebrows at his daughter. "And even though it won't take long, it apparently isn't much fun for a nine-year-old to sit quietly for an hour."

Cora recalled the conversation she'd just had with Bella and decided to take a chance. "They're just about to do a holiday story time hour at the bookstore. I can take her if you want?"

Georgie's eyes lit up at the suggestion. "Oh yes, Daddy, can I go?"

Phil frowned and did his best to ignore Georgie's excited pleas. "I don't want to impose…"

Cora just brushed away his concerns. "I didn't take a lunch break today, and my assistant can cover the counter for a bit. It's a slow day anyway. The holiday rush is mostly over now if you can believe it."

"Please, Dad?" Georgie looked up at him hopefully.

"Only if you're sure—"

"We're sure!" Cora and Georgie said in unison.

"In fact, if we don't hurry, we might just miss the Christmas cookies!" Cora took Georgie's mitten-covered hand in her own, deciding to send a quick text to Natalie when she got to the bookstore.

"Okay, then. I'll be quick. *Behave*," he said to Georgie.

"And have fun!" Georgie finished for him.

Cora could only shake her head. Georgie was only nine and she was already giving her father a run for it. She could only imagine how things would be in a few years.

If he was anything like her father, left to raise not one, but four teenage daughters on his own…Phil didn't stand a chance.

"I think this will be a lot more fun than sitting with your dad while he works," Cora said.

"Did your dad work all the time too?" Georgie asked.

Cora thought about it. Her father and her Uncle Steve had inherited Conway Orchard long before she was born, and her dad was there seven days a week back when he still ran it. She'd never considered it work, though, because it had never taken him away from her. It was a family business. They were all included when it came to picking and harvesting, and each of her sisters and cousins had a wine blend named after them.

"Adults have a lot of responsibilities," Cora told her. "I work a lot too."

"Yes, but you have a fun job!" Georgie insisted. "That's different."

Cora laughed. It was true; she was lucky to do what she loved. And so far, she didn't get the sense that Phil loved what he did, it was just something that was important to him. But was it the most important?

Maybe not, considering he *had* caved to Georgie's request. He just might not know it yet.

They hurried back to the bookstore, joining a few other children and their parents who were coming in for today's event, most of whom Cora knew, of course. There were very few new faces in town other than tourists or summer people, and she'd grown up with nearly everyone who still resided here. Some of her former classmates looked on with curiosity but said nothing. It would be just like the Christmas lady to bring a little girl over for a holiday story hour, after all.

Still, Cora wondered just what kind of business could be so pressing. Just before she stepped inside the bookstore, she looked down Main Street to see Phil walk into the real estate office. She bit her lip to hide her smile. So maybe Phil was starting to see the charm in this small town, after all. Maybe, a long holiday visit would lead to something more.

*

Phil walked into the local real estate office for the appointment he'd scheduled with Lanie Thompson. She hadn't been shy about the fact that she was happy he had pushed back the meeting from Thanksgiving weekend to today.

"The holidays are a big thing around here," she said again now as she led him down the hall and into a small office. She closed the door and gestured to a chair.

"I've noticed," he said as he took a seat opposite her desk. "My daughter is certainly enjoying the experience."

"And you're from Chicago," she said, reviewing her notes. She glanced at his ring finger, and he stifled a grin.

"Only here for the holidays," he said firmly.

His gut tightened on the words though. It was easy to get caught up in the way of life here. It had happened before and it was happening again. But his days were numbered, and there was no sense in leading anyone to believe otherwise.

Lanie gave a look of disappointment. "A shame." Catching herself, she said, "I mean, about your grandparents not coming back to town. They loved it here so much. They were such a big part of the community."

Phil didn't deny this, and he pushed aside the guilt he felt over what his grandparents had lost.

"My grandfather requires around-the-clock care and it's easier for them both to be where they are."

Lanie nodded. "Well, they're certainly missed."

Yes, Phil was beginning to see that. He was also beginning to see why, despite what his father had always said about this town being too quiet and slow-paced, his grandparents saw something more in it, even if more was less in their minds.

"So you're the executor of your grandparents' estate," Lanie said, looking at him expectantly.

"Yes," Phil assured her. He had full legal authority to do what he wished with the properties.

The question he was starting to ask himself was, what would they wish? They'd come to love the cottage just as much as the house on Main, but even after they'd downsized, they couldn't part with the big Victorian. What made him think it would be any easier now?

Nonsense, he told himself. They were past that point in life, and they wouldn't be coming back to town. Holding onto the Main Street property would be sentimental, and that was bad business as far as he was concerned. It wasn't about what he wished. It was about what was best, logically speaking, and doing what needed to be done.

"And you wish to sell both properties?" Lanie clarified.

There was that word again. Was it just him, or did she raise an eyebrow?

Silence stretched. Phil wasn't stupid enough to think that in a town this small, word wouldn't travel. And Lanie looked to be around Cora's age, or close enough that they would know each other. Chances were high that like everyone else in town, Lanie had attended the tree-lighting ceremony as well as the gingerbread event and had seen them together.

Still, this was a professional meeting, and he was a client. In his experience, that meant this discussion didn't leave these four walls.

"There's no reason to hold onto them, as far as I am aware, unless you think there is financial incentive to renting them both out long term?"

Gathering all the facts, he told himself, just like he would in any business transaction. Still, he held his breath as he waited for an answer to the question.

"Well, I don't know how much the holiday shop is paying for rent…" Lanie shuffled some papers on her desk.

Phil did. And he knew it wasn't worth his while to collect that amount if he could sell for more. The small apartment upstairs was a poor use of the space. To his understanding, the remainder of the second-floor space was vacant.

"But here are some sales comps for both properties." Lanie slid two sheets of paper across to him. "As you can see, the property on Main Street has a lot of potential. I always have people looking for a prime location for a small inn."

"And the cottage?" he asked, trying not to place too much importance on the commercial property, even though he knew he was just kidding himself.

"It's waterfront, which helps. I'd need to see the condition, if there are any upgrades that would make sense, but to answer your question, both will sell quickly. The cottage will likely sell to someone from the city looking for a seasonal vacation home. If you list them both in January, I can probably have them both under contract before March."

"That soon?" From their original call, he'd expected to get things underway, but he hadn't expected the closure to come so abruptly.

Lanie smiled proudly. "You came to the right agent. I'm the best in the county."

She was, and he'd known that when he made the appointment with her originally. Only back when he'd made the appointment, he was sitting in his corner office in the West Loop of Chicago, checking an item off his to-do list.

Now, everything felt muddled and permanent. And selling the properties wasn't about scratching off another task.

It was about losing something. For good. And he wasn't so sure how he felt about that anymore.

Only one thing was for sure. If he wanted to go through with selling the property on Main Street, he'd have to tell Cora, and soon.

*

Georgie listened to the Christmas story with rapt attention, more than once causing Bella to give Cora a wink as she turned the page in the picture book. It was an old classic, one that Cora knew by heart, of course, and she turned to Georgie when they finally reached the end.

"Have you heard that story before?"

"Sure I have! But not since last Christmas!" Georgie flashed her a grin and lined up behind the other children who were eager to grab a sugar cookie from the tray before they were gone.

"She's a sweet kid," Bella said, scooting up beside Cora.

Cora suppressed a smile. She could only assume that one of her sisters had either told Bella directly or that one of their mutual cousins had. It had been a long time since Cora was seen even talking with any eligible guy other than Bart, after all. She had reason to assume that bets had already been placed on when they would finally get together.

"They're visiting for the season," Cora said. "Georgie is actually the Keatons' great-granddaughter!"

Bella raised her eyebrows. "Well, now that you say it, I see the family resemblance in the eyes."

"Beautiful eyes," Cora murmured, and then, catching herself, she cleared her throat. "I mean, doesn't she? Georgie, I mean?"

Bella just pressed her lips together and said pertly, "I heard from Maddie the father is rather handsome too."

Cora blushed. There was no sense in denying that, and no reason to either. Bella was a friend, bordering on family, and besides, there was Phil coming through the door now, looking exactly as handsome as Bella had claimed.

"Daddy!" Georgie waved him over and crammed the rest of her cookie into her mouth. "We read a Christmas story and a Christmas song, and there were even Christmas cookies!"

Phil laughed as he brushed some crumbs from the corners of her mouth. "I can see that! Did you save any for me?"

Cora chimed in, "You just missed them, I'm afraid." She motioned to Bella, saying, "This is Bella Clark, she owns the store, and she also happens to be an almost cousin of mine."

Phil looked perplexed. "Almost cousin?"

"We share cousins," Bella explained. "I'm on the mother's side of the family. Cora is on the father's side." She extended her hand. "My sister Natalie also works at Harbor Holidays during the busy season."

"I see," Phil said, grinning at Cora in a way that made her stomach roll over and her heart begin to speed up. "It certainly seems that everyone in Blue Harbor is connected somehow."

"That's small-town life for you." Cora pulled in a sigh, noticing that Bella was giving her one of those subtle looks. A look that said that Cora should try to drag out this social opportunity a little but longer. She should probably get back to the shop, but it wasn't pressing. And she had spent such a lovely hour here with Georgie in this cozy room.

A room that was beginning to feel a little warm now as she took her coat from the hook and shrugged it on.

A parent of a little boy that Cora recognized as a fan of her North Pole model train set pulled Bella into a conversation about gift ideas for her husband, leaving Cora, Phil, and Georgie alone near the front door. Once Georgie was securely bundled in her winter gear, Phil held open the door, letting them both pass through.

It was still early in the day, and Cora had the impression that Phil wasn't exactly sure how to entertain his daughter for the rest of the afternoon.

"There's a skating rink set up in the town square," she mentioned, hoping that her tone came across more casual than eager. She was the Christmas lady, just as Georgie had said.

A Christmas lady with an undecorated and unlit tree in her living room. She couldn't help it; until she knew where it came from, it didn't really feel like hers. Still, she knew that she would decorate it soon. Perhaps even tonight, that was, if she wasn't too tired from a few laps around the rink…

"They still do that?" Phil grinned fondly. "My grandfather took me one time. I'll never forget it."

"Of course they still do it," Cora said. "It's tradition."

"Blue Harbor has a lot of those, I'm noticing," he said, before quickly adding, "Not that I'm complaining."

"My, my, we may just get you into the spirit of things after all," Cora said, and without any further discussion, they walked toward the town square together.

The gazebo was wrapped in garland secured by bright red bows, and Mrs. Knorr was standing beside a make-shift booth, a pile of skates behind her.

"Cora, lovely to see you, dear," she said warmly.

Cora knew that Mrs. Knorr had once been good friends with the Keatons, but she wasn't sure if Mrs. Knorr had ever met Phil, or would even recognize him, given how many years it would seem it had been since he'd been back to town.

"This is Phil and Georgie Keaton," she said by way of introduction.

Mrs. Knorr's face lit up in recognition. "Phil Keaton! Why, I recognize you! Well, it's been years of course. My husband and I often traveled the week you would come to town in the summer, as luck would have it. But you came for Christmas one year..."

Phil cleared his throat. "Yes. Once."

Cora glanced at him, noticing the frown line between his eyebrows that had replaced the earlier light in his eyes. "Well, this is Georgie's first Christmas here in Blue Harbor, and I think she's eager to skate!"

Mrs. Knorr smiled at the little girl and collected their shoe sizes before handing over the skates.

"Be careful, Georgie," Phil warned, as Georgie hurried onto the ice.

She turned and gave him a funny look. "I know how to skate, Dad. I've taken lessons before."

Phil frowned as they watched Georgie skate off, sure on her feet, a smile on her face.

"I didn't know she took lessons," he said quietly.

Cora set a hand on his arm, hoping she wasn't being overly familiar, and liking the sensation of his close proximity to her. "It can't be easy living so far away from her most of the time."

"No," Phil said, closing his eyes briefly, "it's not. But if I'm being honest, I didn't notice a lot of these things even when we lived in the same house. I was just starting my company, and, well…"

"Starting a business takes a lot of time and effort. I understand, and I'm just running a holiday shop," she said.

"Don't sell yourself short," he said. He looked at her for a minute. "Any business is an investment."

Cora finished tying her laces and stood up. "For me, it was an easy one. My mother left us each a small amount of money. There was no better use for my share than a shop dedicated to the season she loved most."

Cora smiled, but Phil didn't match it. He was looking out, over the ice, frowning.

Cora followed his gaze, wondering if Georgie had slipped or gotten hurt. But she was practicing a spin now, oblivious to the two adults making their way onto the slick surface.

Cora didn't realize until her feet came out from under her that she was seriously out of practice. She whooped out loud and felt Phil's steadying hands right before she could hit the hard ice.

"Thank you," she said, laughing at herself to cover her embarrassment.

"I seem to have a way of catching you right before you fall," he said, grinning at her as she righted herself.

True, very true. Only this time around, there wasn't a sprig of mistletoe over their heads.

"Believe it or not, I'm a very good skater," Cora said when Georgie came over to see all the fuss.

"I suppose you have to be, right? Part of all those traditions."

Was it just her, or did Phil's eyes glimmer with amusement?

"That's true, and there are plenty more traditions where that came from," she said pertly, as she found her footing and began to glide alongside Georgie.

Phil made a good show of keeping up with them, but it was clear he was struggling.

"Like what?" Georgie asked excitedly.

"Oh, like…Christmas shopping," Cora said. She hadn't even started shopping for her sisters yet, or her cousins. She supposed she'd have to think about what Candy might like, too.

She sighed. Gifts in her family were carefully chosen and sentimental. Did she really know Candy well enough to know just what she might like?

Sadly, if she didn't, that might just be her doing.

"Oh, shopping." Phil looked stricken. "Yes, I suppose that is a very important tradition."

Sensing he might need a little help in that department, Cora took a breath and offered, "I'm going shopping Sat-

urday afternoon. If you guys want to join me. I know all the best spots in town."

Phil grinned. "It's a date."

Cora winked at Georgie, who skated off happily.

A date, Cora thought, fighting off the smile that made her heart beat just a little faster. And just in time for Christmas.

9

It wasn't like Cora to rely on an assistant quite so much, especially with Christmas being less than two weeks away. But then, it also wasn't much like Cora to have social plans that didn't include one of her sisters or cousins, either.

"You sure you don't mind?" she said to Natalie as she wound her scarf around her neck.

Natalie laughed. "You sound like a new mother about to leave her baby behind so she can get her nails done. I was the same way when Zoe was born."

Cora gave her a rueful grin. "This store is my baby. It's more than that, even. It's…well, it's everything to me."

"All the more reason to go do something nice for yourself. You work hard. And the store will be fine. I do know what I'm doing, you know." Natalie's look was pointed.

It was true. Natalie had excellent customer service skills from her more permanent job at the big hotel on Evening Island. She knew all the merchandise, and where it was located, and could field any questions someone might have.

Cora felt the tension in her shoulders relax. "Thanks. And you know where to reach me if you get swamped."

"Anything exciting planned?" Natalie asked as Cora finished sliding on her gloves and straightening a few displays.

She skirted her eyes, focusing instead on setting up a few of the holiday-themed stuffed animals in an open toy chest. She was doing something exciting today. Something thrilling, really. And out of character. And she didn't want to get too ahead of herself considering that Christmas was less than two weeks away and that it would be the last day that Phil would be in town.

Still, her stomach fluttered when she stood up. "Oh, just a little shopping."

Natalie rolled her eyes. "Don't remind me."

"Still have to tend to Santa's list?" Cora knew that Natalie's seven-year-old daughter was the light of her life.

"Oh, she's easy," Natalie said, with a brush of her hand. "No, I still have to buy for my sisters. Bella is easy because I always get her something related to literature, but Heidi is trickier. And of course, I need to get something for my mother, and she never uses anything I buy her. Last year, she regifted one of my gifts to her to Aunt Miriam! Like I didn't notice! She tried to say it was because she liked it so much that she thought her sister would too, but I knew better." Catching Cora's eyes, she clapped a hand over her mouth, her eyes wide in horror.

"Oh my, Cora," she pleaded, swallowing hard. "I'm sorry. I wasn't thinking. That was so insensitive of me."

Cora brushed away her apology. "Please. I've listened to my friends and cousins talk about their mothers for years now. You shouldn't feel uncomfortable."

"I know, but—" Natalie looked on the verge of tears.

"My mother has been gone for nearly half my life," Cora told her matter-of-factly. "Please don't tiptoe around me."

Natalie pulled in a steadying breath. "Let me at least make it up to you."

Cora gave her a little smile. "You already are. I opened this store because my mother loved the holidays, and it was my way of honoring her. The fact that you love it as much as I do is the best thing I could have hoped for from any assistant."

Natalie grinned. "Too bad you don't need me full time. But then, I do like island life eight months of the year, and the ferry ride is a good way to scout out eligible men."

Cora laughed. Unlike herself, Natalie wasn't quiet about her hunt for a romantic partner.

"And if I might make a suggestion? You can't go wrong with a small, simple, thoughtful gift. Why not give your mother a new ornament each year? Then whenever she hangs it, she'll think of you."

Natalie shook her head, looking as pleased as she was baffled. "You really understand Christmas, Cora."

"I just wish everyone did," Cora said, thinking of Phil. "You know that the Keatons' great-granddaughter wished to spend Christmas here in Blue Harbor? Most kids would have wished for a dollhouse or a new bike."

"Ah, yes, my sister mentioned that you took that little girl to story time. So that's why you needed me to cover for you," Natalie added ruefully.

Cora felt her cheeks warm. "I'm sorry—"

"Don't apologize!" Natalie cried. "I think it's exciting."

Cora didn't reply, even though it was true. It *was* exciting. More often she sat back and watched everyone else fall in love, wondering if someone was ever going to come her way or if she should just listen to her sisters and give Bart a chance at something more than friendship.

"She made the wish on this?" Natalie motioned to the snow globe on the counter and then motioned to Cora. "Now's your chance."

Cora held her breath and then shook her head. "I'm afraid I already used up my Christmas wish."

Natalie leaned into the counter with interest. "Oh, really? And what did you wish for, if I might ask? It wouldn't have anything to do with the handsome man and his cute little girl that we are currently discussing?"

Oh no. Cora wasn't going to spill that easily. "My wish is between me and Santa," she said cheekily.

And on that note, she really should be going. With a skip of her heart, she straightened two more display tables, and let Natalie shoo her out of the shop, all but locking the door closed behind her.

Cora walked next door to the tree lot, where sure enough, Phil and Georgie were already waiting for her.

"You look…festive," Phil observed, his gaze flicking to her red scarf and matching hat.

She smiled up at him. "I didn't know that word was in your vocabulary."

He chuckled. "It wasn't. Until recently."

Their gazes locked for a few, heart-pounding seconds until Georgie wedged herself between them and insisted, "Come on, guys! I don't want to miss seeing Santa!"

Cora knew that there was little chance of that happening, but still, she understood the anxiety. She could still remember feeling the same exact way, when she was a little older than Georgie was now, when her mother first got sick. Christmas wishes were the most magical, her mother had always said, and Cora was counting on the big guy to grant her this one gift.

She'd waited eagerly in the long line, and didn't even complain, but her stomach knotted every time she glanced at the clock and saw that time was winding down, and Santa might have to get back to the North Pole soon. When it was finally her turn, she was almost in tears, so desperate was she to tell Santa what she needed this Christmas. Not a doll, or a board game, or even a new bike, which was a fairly standard gift in Blue Harbor where most people pedaled around town once the snow melted. All she wanted for Christmas was for her mother to get better.

It was the first time her Christmas wish hadn't come true.

She hoped it was the last.

They stopped in a few shops, where Phil discreetly purchased gifts for Georgie and ran them out to the car, while Cora distracted the little girl with some pretty options or her opinion on gifts for her sisters. By the time they were headed to see the big guy, Cora had scratched everyone off her list—except for Candy. Despite the advice she'd given Natalie earlier, she was still coming up blank on what to buy for this new woman in their lives.

"Do you have your list?" Cora tried to keep her tone light as they walked down the street, but her heart ached, despite the company she kept. It came with the territory, she knew. Christmas always made her think of her mother a little more than usual—mostly with a smile, but sometimes not.

"I sure do!" Georgie pulled out a piece of paper that had illustrations along with words. Lots of words.

Cora nudged Phil, feeling a thrill at the physical proximity. "That's a long list."

His eyebrows shot up. "Don't I know it? And here I thought staying in Blue Harbor for the holiday was all you wanted for Christmas," he teased Georgie.

"I need to tell Santa where I'm going to be, so he doesn't go to Mommy's old house in California. That would be a *disaster*."

They had reached the toy store by now and managed to wedge their way into the door. Inside, a line of people had already formed, most of them former classmates, most a few years older, all of whom had found love in this small town, settled down, and started families.

It was possible, she reminded herself. She could almost hear her mother's words. *Anything is possible, Cora, especially at Christmas.*

The line moved quickly, not that Cora minded waiting. Everyone was sandwiched together, so fewer people had to stand outside in the cold, and more than once she had the perk of Phil's body pressing against her. The heat of his proximity made her senses go on high alert and she let the feeling linger, not wanting to inch away.

Did he feel it too? She didn't dare look him in the eye.

Eventually, their turn came up, and Cora was pleased to see that old Mr. Davidson had worked hard on growing his beard this year. He always trimmed it back during the spring and summer, partly because he didn't want to give away his cover and partly because Mrs. Davidson apparently liked a cleanly shaven face. His suit was the same velvet costume he sported every year since she was small enough to sit on his knee, complete with gold embroidered tassels and polished boots.

His kind blue eyes sparkled as Georgie walked over to him, her outgoing demeanor suddenly turning a little shy.

Santa patted his knee, but he looked relieved with Georgie sat beside him on the tufted bench instead. She wasn't exactly a toddler, and Cora was pleased to see that she still believed.

And that Scrooge here hadn't told her otherwise, she thought, glancing at Phil.

"Now," Santa said kindly. "I don't think I'm used to seeing you here in Blue Harbor. Remind me again where you usually come to visit me?"

"Usually in California," Georgie told him.

"Ah, yes, that's right. And what brings you all the way here?"

"I'm spending the holidays here," Georgie told him. "With my dad."

Mr. Davidson glanced at Phil and then shifted his gaze to Cora, giving her a little smile of approval.

Cora felt her cheeks flush.

"And what would you like for Christmas this year? A new doll? Perhaps…a bike?"

Georgie studied the list in her hand and bit at her bottom lip. "I have a list…but if I just ask for one really special thing, do you think it will happen?"

Santa gave a little glance at Phil again, whose nod was almost imperceptible.

"I think that can be arranged. Now, let me see that list." He skimmed it over, commenting on her excellent choices, and then handed it back. "You hold onto that. Or maybe let your dad hold onto it. I have it all stored right here." He tapped his head.

Georgie giggled.

"Now, before you go, why don't you tell me what that one special gift is?"

Georgie carefully tucked her list back into her pocket and then leaned over to whisper in Santa's ear. Cora watched as Mr. Davidson's expression changed, his brow knitting for a moment before he gave Georgie a kind smile.

"That's all I *really* want for Christmas," Georgie said as she stood up.

"Think we'll ever know what it was that she asked for?" Phil asked as he led them out of the store through the side door.

"If you don't find out, I can always ask the big guy." She grinned at Phil. "He and my dad play poker once a month."

Phil laughed. "I might hold you to it. Now, where to next?"

Cora tried to think of a place that would capture all the holiday memories she cherished so much and said, "Is it too cold for ice cream?"

*

Like every other establishment in Blue Harbor, Harborside Creamery had been transformed into a winter wonderland, and the menu reflected the season. Cora usually went for the frozen hot chocolate or the peppermint sundae, but she had a feeling Georgie would prefer the double scoop snowman sundae, complete with an edible top hat made from a chocolate-dipped marshmallow.

"Look, there's even a topping bar over near the back wall if you want to add some sprinkles for snowflakes."

Georgie ran off without needing further encouragement and Phil and Cora settled into a table near the window.

"Georgie's having a good time. Thank you. Between us, I didn't know how I was going to keep her happy this holiday. Being a single parent is challenging."

Cora nodded. "My dad struggled after my mother died. He never complained, and he tried not to show it, but I know it couldn't have been easy for him. Especially at the holidays."

"Is that why you took over?" Phil asked.

Cora thought about this. "Partly. But it helped me to hold onto something, and, well, it helped my dad too, I'd like to think." She gave a little smile. "It's funny that all kids really want is to please their parents." Even though her mother was gone, she still felt that way.

Phil gave a knowing look. "It doesn't always come easy. At least, not for me."

Cora tipped her head, letting him talk.

"My dad had high expectations of me. I'm afraid I still haven't lived up to them yet," he said with chagrin.

"But you have a successful job! A beautiful daughter." Not to mention his other notable attributes, not that she'd be flattering him with those opinions just now. "One that is having the time of her life, in case you haven't noticed. And it's all thanks to you."

"I wish I could take credit for it, but I don't think I can." He gave her a meaningful look until she was forced to look away. She could feel her earlier blush returning, damn it!

"Georgie mentioned that she usually spends Christmas with her mother," Cora said, hoping that she wasn't prying too much. Georgie spoke openly about her mother, and her life, but Phil was definitely more private about things.

Phil nodded, and then shrugged his shoulders. "It's true. When my ex moved out to California, we had an agreement that we'd share the holidays. But the first holiday that was supposed to be mine, I had a business emergency that required me to be out of town. Couldn't let the deal fall apart." He paused for a moment, his mouth tensing. "Long story short, after more legal battles, Georgie has stayed with her mother for the majority of the time. I've been able to get out to California for a couple of long weekends, and Georgie has flown out for a school break or a few days each summer, too."

"That doesn't sound like a lot of time," Cora said, frowning.

Phil arched his eyebrows. "It's not, and it hasn't been easy. My work is demanding. It's definitely been difficult to balance with a personal life. Having Georgie halfway across the country hasn't made things any easier."

Cora smiled. "Well, at least she'll be closer now that her mother is moving back to the Midwest."

Phil's smile was tight. He didn't say anything as he scooped more ice cream onto his spoon.

"Daddy?" Georgie appeared beside him, the evidence of a melted ice cream snowman on her mouth and chin. "I'm hungry."

Phil slanted a glance at Cora, who tried not to giggle. "Hungry? You just ate a sundae."

"Yes, but now I'm hungry for real food. Like, dinner."

Phil's entire expression went blank. "I was supposed to swing by the grocery store today."

"For more of those microwavable meals?" Georgie cried, loud enough for more than one patron to hear and turn to stare.

Cora sputtered on her last spoonful of ice cream. Phil's ears had gone red now.

"Well, for other things too. It's Saturday night. There are places in town to eat. How does that sound?"

"I want to be near the Christmas tree," Georgie said. "Before you know it, it has to come down."

"Tell me about it. I still haven't decorated mine yet." She glanced at Phil, feeling her heart speed up.

Georgie looked at her with surprise. "I thought you didn't have a tree?"

Cora shrugged. "Well, someone thought I needed one."

"I can help!" Georgie exclaimed. "We can order pizza and help, right, Dad?"

Cora slid her eyes to Phil who was giving her a funny look. "I happen to know a thing or two about decorating trees, thanks to this Christmas lady I met," he said. His smoky eyes glimmered. "And I do think you were the one who said that decorating a tree is something that should be shared, not done alone?"

Despite the ice cream, Cora felt as warm inside as if she'd just drank a mug full of hot chocolate. "Okay then!"

It was, as Phil might call it, a date.

*

With Phil's assistance and Georgie's advice, they selected ornaments from the store and carried them upstairs to the bare tree that was waiting in Cora's front window. Phil made a call for the pizza while Cora and Georgie strung the lights, and Cora opened a bottle of wine while Phil turned on the Christmas music.

When he caught her look of surprise, he said, "I figured you'd want some background music. You know, to set the mood."

She couldn't hide her grin. He was getting in the spirit of things, and not just playing along for Georgie's sake.

"Won't you need to sell all these ornaments in the store?" Georgie asked as they unboxed a collection of Nutcracker-themed ornaments.

Cora laughed away the concern. "I have so much merchandise, that I don't need to worry. Besides, this is one of the perks of owning a holiday shop."

"Did you always want to own a shop?" Phil asked from the other side of the tree.

"It wasn't something I'd thought of specifically," Cora admitted. She tried to remember what she'd ever wanted to do with her life and couldn't remember back that far. Once her mother got sick, she stopped looking to the future, she supposed. "I just knew that I loved the way Christmas made me feel. It brought out the best in my family, and in this town, and it was something that I wanted to hold onto, all year long. Having that shop made it possible."

Phil didn't say anything to that, but then, she supposed a guy who didn't bother to celebrate the holiday most years wouldn't understand.

But his grandparents did.

"When I told your grandmother that I wanted to open a holiday shop, she was thrilled. Her enthusiasm was actually what gave me the confidence to go through with it."

Phil arched an eyebrow, as if surprised by this, but then gave a little smile. "She did always love Christmas."

"You didn't want to spend the holiday with them this year?" Cora asked. Even though she hated the thought of

Phil and Georgie leaving town early, she didn't like the thought of the Keatons being alone for Christmas either.

Phil looked momentarily taken aback. "I never…I mean, well, I'm usually working on Christmas, and…I guess I figured that they were used to being on their own for the day."

"Oh, they were never on their own," Cora said pleasantly. She gestured to the window, where the lights from Main Street twinkled in the dusk. "They had an entire community to share it with."

Sensing that she had touched upon a sensitive topic, she said, "But I'm sure they have a new community now, if that facility is as nice as you say it is."

"Not as nice as Blue Harbor," Phil admitted sheepishly.

"Very few places are," Cora said kindly. She reached for another box of ornaments and popped it open. "But then, other than Evening Island, I don't really get out much."

"The shop keeps you that busy?" Phil asked.

Cora considered this. There were some weeks of the year where she had no business at all. The gap between Valentine's Day and Easter was the slowest, and September was slow, too. "The tourists keep things very busy in the summer, actually."

"Good, that's good."

"Good for me. And good for your grandparents," Cora said with a laugh.

It was on the tip of her tongue to ask about the cottage and his plans for it. He hadn't mentioned visiting the real estate office the other day and she wasn't one to pry. But if the Keatons weren't returning to town and if Georgie loved it here so much, wouldn't it make sense for Phil to consider buying the place for himself, for weekends and summers?

The doorbell rang, interrupting her thoughts, and Phil went downstairs to collect the pizza.

"Back door," Cora informed him. "Everyone knows the front door is only for the shop."

"Good to know," Phil said in a way that made Cora think he was stowing that bit of information aside, just like a local would.

They ate their pizza on the floor, under the Christmas tree, and Cora had to admit that after experiencing a tree all of her own, she'd never go back on that again.

And maybe, she thought, glancing at the two new people in her life, she wouldn't have to.

"Oh!" she said, jumping up. "We forgot the most important part."

She left her curious guests in the living room and hurried downstairs to the shop, where the angel tree topper was resting on the top branch of a medium-sized tree near the counter. Standing on her tip toes, she carefully brought it down. She held it close, feeling protective, and revealed it proudly once she was back inside.

"We can't finish the tree without the angel. Georgie, do you want to do the honors?"

Georgie carefully took the tree topper from Cora, and Phil hoisted her up until the angel was standing tall and proud on the top of the tree.

"It's right where it belongs," Cora said aloud. Immediately, she felt her cheeks flush. "Sorry," she said, slanting a glance at Phil. "It just wouldn't feel like Christmas without that angel on top of a tree."

"It wouldn't feel like Christmas without a lot of things, this night included," Phil said quietly.

His gaze roamed her face, and for a moment, the entire room seemed to fall silent.

Until a well-known children's carol came on the radio and Georgie began to sing along, at high volume.

"Well," he said, clearing his throat. "I should probably get Georgie home to bed."

Georgie let out a groan of protest. "But I don't want the fun to end!"

Me either, kid, Cora wanted to say. Instead, she fell back on her old habit to find something to look forward to. This time it was easy.

"But did you know that the Winter Carnival is just a few days away? It all kicks off Friday night. There are games and music and food."

"And snow?"

Cora laughed. "I hope!" Though she knew that even if by some strange chance the snow were to melt between now and then, Bart would bring in his snow machine and put it to good use. "This far north, the chance of the snow melting before March is pretty slim. The important part is that it started before Christmas, so it will be here to stay. What's Christmas without snow?"

"Try living in California," Georgie grumbled.

Cora gave Phil a wry grin as they put back on their coats. "Thank you. For the pizza. And…for tonight."

"Consider it an early Christmas gift," he said with a wink.

10

Phil had taken Georgie to dinner at most of the inns that lined Main Street, along with the pizza parlor, but tonight Georgie wanted to try the Firefly Café next to the bakery. Phil wavered, knowing that Cora's sister owned the place, but then told himself that maybe this was a good thing. Maybe he could learn a little more about the proprietor of the holiday shop, see if there was any chance of making this entire situation better than it was turning out to be.

Though looking at his daughter's face as she stared at the lights of Main Street, he wasn't sure how he could top this.

"Can we come back here again this summer so you can teach me how to fish?" Georgie asked as they made their way down the side street toward the small building that housed the bakery and café.

Phil didn't want to crush his daughter's spirit, even though the answer should be a simple one. This summer he'd be overseas, something he'd been planning for a long time, something he'd been excited about…until now. Usually, he lived for the rush that came with each new business deal, long after he'd had enough money in his bank account to make it worth his while. But now he felt that same rush every time Georgie laughed, or took his hand, or gave him a hug goodnight.

He was bonding with his daughter. Basking in her love. And he was falling for a kind, beautiful woman.

Wasn't this all that most people needed out of life?

Not his father, he reminded himself. He'd scorned that way of life in his parents and he would do so in Phil, too. Growing up it had all been about the accomplishment, not the effort. Didn't matter if Phil played a good game on the soccer field. What mattered was that they'd won. Didn't matter that Phil sat alone on Christmas, or in a stuffy restaurant, bored and lonely. He'd gotten that expensive new video game system, hadn't he?

Eventually, the desire to please his father, to connect with him, had morphed into his own way of life.

But here was his daughter, his child, just trying to connect with him.

In the simplest of ways.

"It's too cold to think about summer just yet," he said, hoping to change the topic. He motioned to the building as they approached, each window framed in lights, the front glass-paned door bearing a wreath made of sleigh bells. "Besides, all I can think about now is food!"

"Me too," Georgie said happily. "Especially since it's not frozen pizza!"

The Firefly Café was, like most places in town, completely decorated for the holidays. Garland, tinsel, lights, wreaths, even a small red and green floral arrangement on each table.

Georgie lapped it up, especially the children's menu, which turned out to be a coloring contest of sorts.

"Every kid who helps me decorate my tree gets a free dessert," the woman who was visibly Cora's sister said when she motioned to the tree covered in paper ornaments, some colored carefully, others not so much.

"I'm an expert at decorating trees," Georgie informed her. "We decorated our own tree and I also helped decorate Cora's tree."

The woman's eyebrows shot up as she glanced at Phil. "Cora happens to be my sister. I'm Amelia," she said warmly, clearly giving him the once-over.

Phil had prepared himself for this. As Cora pointed out—it was a small town. He couldn't hide his friendliness with Cora any more than he could have hidden the fact that he was the Keatons' grandson.

"Phil Keaton," he said. "And my daughter, Georgie."

"I heard that you were related to the Keatons! Sorry, word travels in small towns," Amelia said apologetically.

Phil chewed the inside of his cheek uneasily, wondering if word of his plans for the properties might have traveled too.

But Amelia just smiled and said, "I love your grandparents. They used to come in here nearly every Saturday night and sit right over there at that table." She gestured to the window. "They're certainly missed."

Phil wasn't quite sure what to say to that. He was pretty certain that his grandparents must miss it here, too, though how would he know? He barely visited. Didn't have time. He'd set them up, paid for their expenses, took over their affairs, much the same way that he had paid for Georgie's private school tuition, sent her expensive gifts, asked his assistant to show her a good time when she came for a visit.

He'd assumed everyone was happy that way, taken care of—that he had made their lives easier, the best way he knew how.

Now, he wasn't so sure.

He wasn't sure of anything.

"Well," Amelia said, "I'm actually heading out early this evening. I'm hosting a Christmas party at my house for some of the ladies in town."

"Not that I was invited," said Candy, as she joined the conversation, pushing close to Amelia. She gave her a mock scolding look.

"I meant for my sisters and cousins—"

"Oh, I know what you meant," Candy said. "But it's fine. It's fine. You young ones need some fun." She eyed Phil meaningfully. "Especially Cora."

Amelia was glowering at Candy now, and Phil hid his smile behind a menu. Being an only child, he missed out on this kind of banter growing up, but then, he supposed that even in his home, his parents rarely joked. They weren't together often enough.

"Well, I have a feeling that Georgie here will make the prettiest ornament on my tree," Amelia said, shifting her attention away from Candy.

"Oh, no doubt," Candy remarked. "Especially if you've been spending time with Cora. She has a way of rubbing off on people."

Amelia leveled her with a look, clearly suppressing a sigh. "She has a way of spreading Christmas cheer, that much is certain."

Candy gave a little mew. "That too."

"Candy, can you please check on the flatbreads in the oven?" Amelia said, a noticeable edge to her tone.

Candy didn't seem to catch it and hurried away, only to say cheerfully, "I'll be back!" over her shoulder before disappearing through a swing door.

Phil set down his menu, deciding to place his order, even if it was just to let poor Amelia have it out with Candy behind the closed kitchen door. "I'll have the pot pie."

"And mac and cheese for Georgie, I'm guessing?" Amelia collected the menus, and Georgie nodded happily. "Those are two of my specialties. I'll make them before I go."

"Oh, don't let us keep you," Phil said. "I'm sure Candy—"

But Amelia just shook her head. "A special friend to my sister is a special guest of mine."

Phil grinned, happy that Candy was out of earshot. No doubt she'd take a comment like that and read into it.

Even if she might not be far off the mark.

*

Cora hadn't seen her sisters since Maddie had broken the news to her about her alternative plans for Christmas Eve, but tonight was their family's annual cookie swap party, and that was one tradition that she knew they wouldn't sacrifice, at least. It was something that their mother and aunt used to do with their friends and neighbors, and as the girls grew older, they were invited to participate. Now, an entirely new generation of women still met one snowy evening in December to drink wine and cider and hot chocolate, and swap cookies and recipes. There was only one rule, and that was that they couldn't bring the same kind of cookie two years in a row.

For Amelia and Maddie, this was a welcome challenge. For Cora, not so much.

She let herself into Amelia's warm house and hung her coat and scarf on the hook, noticing that most of the guests had already arrived by the number of boots lined up on the mat. She added hers to the mix and walked into the living room, where her sisters, cousins, and their cousins were either gathered around the fireplace, or visible in the adjacent kitchen.

"Merry Christmas!" she said, feeling the anticipation of a fun night ahead. The Christmas tree was small and simply decorated, but it was still beautiful, and from the mantel hung two stockings, no doubt for her and Matt, even if he lived at the house he'd purchased when he returned to town over the summer.

"Get a glass of wine and join us!" Bella called over cheerfully. On the coffee table was a whole spread of snacks, compliments of Amelia no doubt, because even though all the girls brought cookies to swap and take home, that didn't mean they ate them at the party.

Well, maybe a few.

Cora walked into the kitchen and set her two boxes of cookies on the table with the others, wondering if her ginger snaps and jam thumbprints would hold up to some of the more ambitious creations that she personally couldn't wait to taste.

"These must be yours," she said to Maddie, who filled them each a glass of wine. There was no doubt that the coconut snowball cookies decorated to perfection to look like the top of a snowman were the work of the baker in the family.

"I'll admit that I did use this year's cookie swap as a way to test some new recipes. Promise you'll give me your honest opinion?"

"Don't I always?" Cora said, which received a little pinch of Maddie's mouth.

Maddie was honest, always. Britt pretty much too. Amelia and Cora being sandwiched in the middle of the sibling order tended to be more inclined to go with the flow and keep the peace.

"Speaking of honesty," Maddie said when Amelia joined them at the table carrying a bowl of what Cora recognized as her famous spinach dip. "How on earth did you pull this all together? You've been at the café since the crack of dawn."

"Candy closed up," Amelia said humbly, even though they all knew just how much work it was to run your own business, plus host a group of women, even if most of them were family and therefore forgiving. "And I would have left earlier if a certain handsome someone hadn't stopped by."

Assuming that her sister meant her boyfriend, Cora said, "Did Matt help set up, then?"

"I was referring to *your* handsome someone, Cora. This was my first proper look at Phil Keaton, and I have to say, he might just be the best Christmas present you've ever received."

Cora felt her cheeks burn. "Please. He's just a…" She didn't know what he was. He wasn't a friend. But he wasn't more than that either. "He's just passing through town. He's just here for the holidays."

But she hoped that wasn't true at all.

So much for honesty.

"Well." Natalie came into the kitchen with Gabby and poured herself a glass of wine. "If you don't want him, you can send him my way."

Cora felt her cheeks flame. She had the sense that Natalie was only half-joking, and her back was against a wall now. She'd have to come clean about her feelings, put her real hopes out there, even if she didn't dare admit them even to herself.

It was Maddie who came to her defense, saying, "Well, I'm just happy that you've found a nice guy, Cora, and at Christmastime, too! It was meant to happen for you of all people at this time of year."

"Of course, we always thought you and Bart would be sort of a cute couple," Gabby said as she reached over and snatched a cookie.

Cora shook her head. "Bart only sees me as a friend."

"You so sure about that?" Gabby raised an eyebrow as she munched on a chocolate-covered gingersnap.

Cora thought about her banter with Bart, the ease, the way he'd carried that tree all the way up to her living room. And never did tell her who sent it.

A thought took hold as her breath caught, and she hoped the other ladies wouldn't notice the emotion in her face. Had it been *Bart* who sent the tree?

Was it possible that there was more there than she'd noticed over the years? She swallowed uneasily.

No, she didn't think so. Bart was a great guy, sweet, and easy to talk to, and good-looking, sure. But she'd never felt any of those warm and tingly feelings for him as she had for Phil.

"And does it matter if he works in Chicago?" Amelia pointed out. "His grandparents have two properties here. Sounds like a very good excuse to get back to town, especially if he's already willing to spend so much time in Blue Harbor right now."

Cora thought back to the visit he'd made to the real estate office, hoping that her sister was right. Amelia was sensible; she wouldn't mislead her or give her false hope.

And she was also voicing exactly what Cora wanted to be true, more than anything else on her Christmas list…or beyond.

11

The week had passed quickly, thanks to it being Cora's busiest week of the year, even busier than next week would be, because usually by Christmas week, most people were only coming in for last-minute gifts or in search of a centerpiece or other themed items for their holiday parties or Christmas dinner.

And, of course, there was the Winter Carnival to think about—usually something that she looked forward to with great anticipation, mostly because her kiosk was always something she spent her summer months planning and dreaming about. Each year she tried to keep it fresh, with new themes and decorations, and this year she had come up with the idea of highlighting various traditions from around the world. She'd special ordered ornaments from Germany to Finland to South America, but as she carefully unboxed the items on Friday afternoon, shivering in her down coat and knowing that thanks to the power strips running along the back of the kiosks, she could turn on her space heater, the anticipation she felt was not for the festivities of the day, but, of course, at the thought of seeing Phil and Georgie.

"Ho, ho, ho," a deep voice rang out across the square, and Cora smiled to herself. Mr. Davidson would be sitting in the big red chair set up in the gazebo for the morning portion of the day, per tradition of course, and already families had lined up all the way to the street corner.

"You're popular around here," Cora told him, as he approached.

"That was a mighty sweet girl you were with last weekend," he remarked.

Cora felt herself swell with pride, even though she could stake no claim in Georgie's life. She was a sweet girl, and a happy one, too. It was obvious that she loved Christmas every bit as much as Cora did.

"She's a girl after my own heart," Cora agreed.

"That she is," Mr. Davidson said. "Single father, huh?"

Cora wasn't sure where he was going with this, but she nodded all the same. "That's right." She knew best what it was like to grow up with one, after all. It hadn't been easy for him, but he'd never complained or let on. She always knew that she and her sisters meant everything to Dennis Conway, and he wasn't shy in making that known either. He encouraged them to each follow their dreams, even if those dreams might have led Britt away for more than a decade. He'd been patient, and kind, and always positive, no matter how difficult their circumstances.

Looking back on things now, as an adult, she knew that her father must have been terribly lonely and overwhelmed after his wife died. But he'd never let on. Everything he had done had been for his children.

And now, the least Cora could do was to repay the favor, even if it meant tolerating Candy a little more, and her unfamiliar traditions.

Still, Cora couldn't often shed the feeling that she had to take care of him, too. That without her, there might not be a Christmas at all—at least not a proper one.

She smiled to herself, thinking that maybe Phil was right. Without her, she wasn't sure how Georgie's Christmas would have turned out either.

"Just between us, do you happen to remember what Georgie asked for when she whispered in your ear?" Cora asked. "The one really special thing she wanted from her Christmas list?"

Mr. Davidson's expression clouded, and for a moment, Cora wondered if he was going to get a little too far into his role and claim that Christmas wishes were top secret.

Instead, he nodded slowly. "It wasn't on the list. She said that she wants to spend more Christmases like this with her father."

Cora fell silent as she processed the magnitude of such a simple request. She could tell that Mr. Davidson was thinking the same thing as her. That of all the things in the world the child could have asked for, she was asking for something that shouldn't really have to be asked for at all.

"Thank you," Cora said, not yet sure what she would do with the information, but knowing that she should find a way to tell Phil, even though she was still a little worried that he might not fully understand. Or worse, take offense. He was sensitive about his relationship with his daughter, even if it had bloomed right before Cora's very eyes. "The father is a bit of a Scrooge, you might say."

"Tourist?"

Cora sighed as she popped open the last box of her ornaments. They were lovely, hand-painted, and representing Italy.

"Actually, he's the Keatons' grandson."

Mr. Davidson squinted at her. "But the Keatons loved Christmas!"

Cora could only shrug. "Guess they didn't pass on the traditions."

Which was exactly why she felt it was so important to keep her own alive. It would break her heart not to keep her mother's thoughtful plans and dreams going. Luckily, thanks to the store, she didn't have to. So long as she could keep sharing the joy of the season, she wouldn't have to worry about her sisters moving on with their lives and holiday plans.

Phil and Georgie were proof of that.

"Don't worry. I'm working on him," she assured Mr. Davidson, and he laughed, a jolly sound, straight from the belly. He was a natural.

"Oh, I never had any doubt."

From across the square, the children had started to notice the plush, deep red, velvet suit, and the signature white curly beard, and a cry went up as they began calling out to him, their excitement growing when he pulled up his belt and then lifted a white-gloved hand in a dramatic wave.

Cora chuckled. "You're good at this."

"You are too," he remarked.

Cora smiled to herself as he walked away. She was good at this. And really, Phil was too. He just had to believe in Christmas. And in himself.

Feeling warmer than she had earlier, even without the assistance of a heater, she waved to Natalie who joined her to finish setting up the stand.

"Be sure to take some time off to enjoy yourself," she told Natalie. Even though they would be busy, this was a special event that she wanted to enjoy.

"Thanks," Natalie replied. She gave Cora a funny look. "I was hoping to enter the skating contest with Zoe. My mom offered, but I don't want her slipping and breaking something."

Cora laughed, thinking of the result of her father's recent fall. "Don't want her ending up with a caregiver like Candy."

"She's not so bad, though, right?" Natalie asked.

Cora thought about it. "Not bad. Just different."

"Different isn't always worse," Natalie said. "And I should know. When I got divorced, I thought my life was over, but Zoe and I have made it work. Being in Blue Harbor helps, even if there aren't many eligible men."

Cora grinned. Not long ago, she was lamenting over this too. Still, Natalie had a point. Different was just different. Not necessarily better or worse. She'd try to remember that next time Candy tried to change the way her family usually did things. It would be a struggle, she knew.

She swept her eyes over the green, which had been covered in a blanket of white snow for weeks now, looking for a glimpse of a red pom-pom hat. Phil wouldn't miss this event! He couldn't. Georgie wouldn't let him.

It wasn't until Natalie had left and returned from the skating contest, a third-place ribbon proudly in her hand, and they had restocked their bestseller, glistening tree toppers shaped like stars, that Cora finally spotted Phil approaching her stand.

Her heart sped up and her stomach flipped and the little jab that Natalie gave her was nearly enough to knock her off her feet, had the snow been any slicker.

"You came!"

"Daddy had to work," Georgie explained. "I hope we didn't miss anything."

"Absolutely not," Cora said, deciding not to mention the skating contest. There would be plenty more activities to keep Georgie happy.

And her happy too, she thought, deciding now was actually a good time to break away. The surge of traffic when the carnival opened had waned in the last hour or so.

"You never stop," Phil remarked. He hesitated before adding, "I was sort of hoping you'd have some free time today. So we could…talk."

Talk? Her heart skipped a beat when she considered the implication. There was something he wanted to tell her.

Her mind wandered back to that visit he'd made to the real estate office. Had he seen the good that being here had done for Georgie? And for himself?

Never mind, she thought, biting her lip.

Natalie raised her eyebrows. All but mouthed, "Go!"

Cora hesitated. In years past, she only ever took a break from the stand to make the rounds, support the other kiosks, and of course grab some cider or hot chocolate to stay warm. But this year, she had too good of an excuse to leave.

"Time for you and Georgie? Of course." She stage-whispered to Georgie, "There's a snowman contest later on and I happen to be an expert snowman maker."

"Why doesn't this surprise me?" Phil laughed again.

The first stop was a warm beverage, complements of Buttercream Bakery, of course. As much as Cora enjoyed chatting with her sisters, she was happy to see that Maddie's assistant was covering things while Maddie picked up the last of her supplies from the storefront. She didn't need any more suggestive glances just now, even though she was sure there would be more to come.

"Do you like to sled?" Cora asked Georgie, as they all sipped steaming cups of thick hot chocolate. They were seated near one of the warming stations, and as reluctant as Cora was to leave behind the cozy feeling she had, seated with Phil and his daughter on a bench, sharing a thick, wool, plaid blanket that they used to cover their legs, she couldn't imagine a better reason than to enter the sledding contest.

"We don't have sledding in California," Georgie said. "And when I visit Daddy, he lives in a big building in the city, and there are only other buildings all around it."

"Well," Cora said, with a knowing smile. "Just a couple blocks behind this town square there happens to be a really big, huge, giant hill."

"Really?" Phil looked at her in confusion, and Cora had to burst out laughing. The tension had officially dissipated and she was thankful for it. She liked this, spending time with Phil and Georgie, showing them her town, and seeing Georgie get nearly as excited as she was as a child.

And she was starting to get the impression that Phil liked it too.

"Oh, that hill!" Phil winked at her, catching on. Really, it was hardly a mountain, but it was steep, and the walk up and down it used to make Cora and her sisters break a sweat through layers of thermal shirts, sweaters, snowsuits, scarves, and hats. The wind in the face as they whisked down to the bottom again made the hike worth it, though.

"There's a sledding competition," Cora said. She checked her phone. "We still have time if we hurry."

"Can we, Dad?" Georgie turned to him excitedly.

"Sounds like fun!" Phil said, standing, and Cora had the impression that he wasn't just saying that on his daughter's behalf.

They trekked through the snow to the back of the festival, and through the wooded path where signs led everyone to the hill. Already, Cora could see a crowd gathering at the top, and she realized with a little laugh that the hill looked even smaller now as an adult.

"It's been a few years since I've done this," she admitted to Phil, who was just shaking his head.

"It's the Midwest," he said. "Not Colorado. Still, look." He jutted his chin to Georgie, whose eyes were wide circles now as she gasped at the sledding hill before her.

He bent down and whispered, "Think you're brave enough?"

She swatted him, the smile never leaving her face. "Let's hurry!"

Cora and Phil stood in line for the sleds while she dashed away. "She reminds me so much of myself when I was that age," Cora said.

"How so?" Phil asked.

"Oh, you know, just a zest for life."

Phil thought about it for a moment. "She doesn't get it from me. I…I never was that way, you know? Guess I'm still not."

"Oh, now," Cora said, not willing to let him off the hook that easily. "You are about to enter Blue Harbor's annual sledding competition. Winner gets a gift certificate to the Carriage House Inn. The pub there can't be beat."

"And the loser?"

"A trip to the hospital for a broken leg?" Cora was only half-joking. There was the year where Mickey Scott greased the bottom of his sled and barely missed hitting a tree.

Phil laughed. "Well, if we win, then it's a date."

Cora felt her cheeks flush, heating her all the way through her chilled hands, and she hid her smile as they reached the front of the line and Phil selected one sled.

"We should all fit on this, eh?"

Cora hadn't known what the logistics would be, but sharing a sled with Phil and Georgie hadn't entered her mind.

"Back when I was a kid, my sisters and cousins and I would all go against each other," she admitted as they moved back toward the hill. Georgie was already at the top, waving with both hands to them.

Phil arched an eyebrow. "Competitive?"

"Only when it comes to sledding," Cora said ruefully.

"Then we'd better win!" Phil grinned, and Cora's stomach did a little swooping movement that made her take a breath.

If a win meant that Phil would stand by his word and take her to dinner at the pub, then yes, they had better win.

"For Georgie," she said, meeting his eye.

"Of course," he said. "For Georgie."

By the time they reached the top of the hill, Cora was panting and out of breath. Her lungs burned and she had a cramp in her side. She caught Phil giving her a strange look, and she laughed. Or rather, wheezed.

"I told you that I haven't done this in a while," she said.

Phil's breath escaped in white clouds. There was a gleam in his eye, and she noticed that he didn't seem remotely winded.

"My daddy has a gym in his building and he likes to do the stairs," Georgie said matter-of-factly.

"I guess I'm spending too much time holed up in my shop," Cora said.

"You ever think of changing it up, scaling back?" Phil posed the question in a serious enough tone that Cora had to look at him properly for a moment.

"Never," she finally said. "I love that shop. It's…my favorite place in all of Blue Harbor. It's…my home."

"It's my favorite place, too," Georgie said firmly.

Cora glanced at Phil one more time to try to understand what he meant by this, but he had already turned away, positioning their sled. Cora shrugged it off, realizing that she was being overly defensive. So she was a homebody. And so she was perfectly content setting up her shop each day. It might not leave much time for the gym or a social life, but it didn't mean that she would trade it for anything.

Well, almost anything, she thought, catching Georgie's smile.

She shook her head when she saw that Phil was setting up the sled in the middle of the pack, putting them at a distinct disadvantage.

Cora cleared her throat, catching his attention, careful not to raise suspicion from some of the more competitive crowd. She eyed her sister Britt and Robbie and Keira at the far end of the hill. Typical. That was always Britt's favorite take-off spot as a kid. But Cora's was different.

With a jut of her chin, she motioned for Phil to follow her back toward the path they'd walked up, where there was always a large bump. Sure enough, it was still there.

"We don't want to go straight down the middle?" Georgie asked.

"Nope," Cora said. "You have to trust me on this."

Georgie gave a big smile. "I trust you."

Phil blinked a few times, looking thrown, and then helped Georgie onto the front of the sled. Cora realized with a jolt that she was expected to sit in the middle, with Phil at the rear.

"If you're willing to do this bobsled style, then we'll really have a fighting chance," Cora said over her shoulder. One glance down the top of the hill confirmed that Britt had the same idea.

"You sure?" But a grin flashed on Phil's face. He was having fun.

Good.

Cora leaned forward to double-check that it would be okay with Georgie. "You don't mind going really fast, do you? And maybe, going in the air a little too?"

"Yeah!" Georgie cried out in delight.

Cora laughed and turned back to Phil. "I'm sure."

The mayor's wife was in charge of blowing the horn, and she stood to the side of the path, in a bright red coat, impossible to miss. Cora tightened her hand on the rope and lifted the heel of her boot onto the sled.

"Hold me tight," Georgie said, the first hint of trepidation sneaking into her otherwise excited voice.

Cora squeezed tighter just as the horn went, and with a giant push they were off, Phil hopping on behind them just before she feared it might be too late. The weight of his body propelled them down the hill, holding them steady, and pushing against her back like a strong, warm blanket. She barely had a moment to revel in the pleasure of the feeling when they approached the bump.

"Here we go!" she cried out, bracing herself as Georgie screamed in excitement and they were hurled into the air just long enough for Cora to fear that this really may not have been a good idea, after all, considering that she was now a grown woman with a lot to lose if she were to injure herself. Never mind Georgie!

But they landed with a thud and Georgie giggled so hard that even Cora was laughing, and she didn't even realize they had won until they'd slid to a far stop and Mayor Hudson himself was running toward them with the iconic plastic trophy.

"You really screamed up there!" Phil said.

"What?" Cora stared at him from the sled where they still sat. "That was Georgie!"

"Sure," he teased. "Blame it on the kid."

She narrowed her eyes, giving him a menacing smile, but she was having fun. Real, genuine fun that she hadn't had in far too long, even though this was the exact feeling that she had tried so hard to capture and hold onto, and keep alive in her shop.

"It's not as easy as when I was Georgie's age," she said as the little girl sprang to her feet and ran to collect their prize.

Cora all but rolled off the sled, struggling to come to her knees, and she was both amused and surprised to see that Phil was doing the same.

"No yoga for you, then, I presume?"

"Please, I can't remember the last time I've had to pull myself up off the floor. Let alone wearing all this." He managed to get up, and Cora tried too, grunting at the effort, and all but slipping on an icy patch.

Phil extended a hand, and gratefully, Cora reached up and took it, catching her breath at how solid and strong it felt as he easily lifted her to her feet. Her only regret was that she was still wearing her darn gloves.

"Can I go see Keira?" Georgie asked.

"Of course," Phil said. "I'll find you in a few minutes. But don't slip!" he added as she tore across the park in her boots, stumbling in the freshly fallen snow.

Cora waited until she had met up with Keira to turn to Phil and say, "I found out what Georgie's Christmas wish to Santa was."

Phil straightened with relief. "Thank goodness, because I haven't been able to figure it out no matter how much I try to get her to tell me." He looked at Cora eagerly. "What is it?"

"She wants to spend Christmas with you again, here in Blue Harbor."

*

Phil sucked in a breath. His heart was beginning to pound just thinking about how he was going to let his little girl down. He'd gotten used to seeing the light in her eyes, the smile on her face. Could he really let it all go now?

Another Christmas in Blue Harbor was impossible. Even another Christmas together wasn't likely, not for a while at least. He pushed back the knot in his throat when he considered how old Georgie would be by the time he'd come back from Europe.

Old enough to lose the spirit she had now, that much was for sure.

Old enough to stop reaching for his hand.

He could always come back. Take a week off, fly home, stay in the corporate apartment. But it would be worse than the Christmas he'd planned to offer her this year. Gray, sterile. No doubt she'd prefer to stay with her mother.

Cora was frowning at him. "What's wrong? I was thinking you'd be flattered."

"That's not a promise that I can make," Phil said. "I'm not going to have Georgie with me next Christmas."

Cora's face fell. "Oh, the custody arrangement. Well, maybe you can tell her something like every other Christmas here in Blue Harbor?"

Phil swallowed hard, knowing that she was handing him an opportunity, that he could tell Cora what he'd come here to do, here and now, only the thought of hurting her was almost worse than the thought of hurting Georgie.

And at the rate things were going, he was going to end up doing just that, to both of them.

"I'm opening an office overseas. I'm going to be away for a while."

"For how long?" Cora asked.

"At least eighteen months, more like two years." He'd been so excited about the prospect of it. Until now. "It's been planned for a while. Long before I knew that Georgie's mother was moving back to the Midwest. And Georgie…she didn't like spending time with me before."

Only he knew that wasn't exactly true. It was more that they'd never spent time together before, not like this, day after day, doing things that brought her joy.

"I find that hard to believe," Cora said.

He swallowed hard. "I wish it was. But she doesn't like my apartment. She's bored on her visits." And he was entirely to blame for that, wasn't he?

"But that's all changed now," Cora pointed out. "It's her Christmas wish to spend more time with you."

Phil sucked in a breath. That was certainly one scenario he hadn't seen coming.

He glanced at Cora. And this was another.

One step at a time, he told himself. One problem at a time. That's how he approached everything in life. Or at least, in his career.

His career that had been all-consuming. Everything to him. Just like his father's was to him.

His father had lost his own parents to that mentality. And he'd never really gained a son, had he?

No matter how hard Phil had tried to win him over.

"I've committed to this. I have people counting on me."

Cora nodded as if she understood, but her eyes said otherwise. He knew what his ex would have said. That his family were people too. That they counted on him, too.

It was the same dilemma, now, then. Always.

He'd assumed that he was doing enough by her, providing for her, leading by example, the way his father had done for him. But it wasn't enough.

"Georgie doesn't know yet," he told Cora now. "I've been waiting for the right time to tell her."

He looked at her, seeing the disappointment in her eyes, and hating it. Hating that he knew the disappointment would be so much worse if he told her everything.

"Well, now you know what she wants more than anything else," Cora said. She avoided looking at him, her expression tight, and Phil didn't know what else to offer her in that moment, or what else to even say, other than the cold hard truth.

"Now I know."

And he knew that despite everything he'd set out to do, things were getting more complicated by the day.

They walked through the festival, stopping to look at various kiosks, saying little until Cora suddenly stopped in her tracks.

"Not to overstep, but is there any chance you might change your mind about going away? For Georgie, of course," Cora added quickly. "You have the house here. Your grandparents loved Blue Harbor. And Georgie does too. And it's not too far from Chicago. A lot of people come up here on weekends, summers…"

They locked eyes for a beat, and Phil didn't quite know what to say, even though she was asking him the very same question that he'd been asking himself since that first full day here in Blue Harbor, when what was supposed to be a weekend trip to tie up his connection to this town turned into something more.

"If only life were that simple," Phil said, hearing the longing in his own voice.

"Can't it be?" Cora shrugged. "My life is pretty simple. I grew up in this small town. I know pretty much everyone, and my days are fairly routine." Her cheeks turned pink for a second and she looked down, her lashes fluttering as she covered her smile with an embarrassed laugh. "My life must sound pretty boring when I describe it that way."

"Not at all," Phil replied honestly. "I was thinking that it actually sounded…nice."

Cora met his eye. He could feel their connection and wondered if she sensed it too. Wondered what she would say if she knew why he'd really come to town in the first place, and why he had been so eager to leave. Why Christmas was nothing but another day on the calendar. Why he'd been willing to leave the country for an extended period of time, with even more limited contact with his only child.

"My life has been pretty complicated," he explained. "Work consumed a lot of my time while I was married." He laughed. "It consumes even more time now that I'm not."

"You have an important job," Cora pointed out.

Phil nodded. "I do. And I take it seriously. But it's like you said, Georgie is counting on me too. I just didn't think she actually wanted to spend time with me, if I'm being honest."

Cora looked at him in shock, and Phil elaborated, "She never liked her visits to my house. Well, my apartment. I tried to make it fun for her, but I guess that take-out food and a movie isn't exactly what she had in mind."

"She's having a wonderful time with you here in Blue Harbor," Cora said.

"I know," Phil said, rubbing a hand over his jaw. "It's given us a chance to connect. It's made me realize things could be different."

A lot different, he thought, glancing at Cora.

"It certainly gives you something to think about," Cora said, giving him a little smile.

His chest tightened on that thought. It certainly had.

12

Cora was especially sad when the Winter Festival came to an end, and not just because it meant she'd have to wait another year for it to come around again, but because now they were just one more day closer toward Phil leaving town.

And maybe not returning.

She didn't know if it was the freshly falling snow or the sounds of the music playing in the background, or the knowledge that Christmas was now just around the corner, but Cora felt a sense of hope that she knew some more cynical people she knew might call denial.

Things had a way of working out at Christmastime. If there was ever a time for magic, this was it.

It was late Saturday afternoon. There would be a bonfire and carols and an evening skate, but the kiosks were closing for the night, leaving behind only the refreshment stands. Typically, she used this time to join her cousins for a much-needed glass of wine and to warm her hands and rest her feet near the bonfire. This was her sister Britt's first year back, but now she was handing out mulled cider and wine, and of course, Amelia and Maddie were selling food, as always. The blessing, she supposed, was that Candy had been asked to help too, meaning there was no chance for her to comment on the time that Cora and Phil had spent together yesterday.

Or what they had discussed.

She finished setting the last of her ornaments into their boxes when she felt someone approach from behind her.

"Need a hand?"

Cora had every reason to be disappointed in Phil, not to mention wary of wanting to get closer to this man, but when she turned and saw the crinkle in his eyes when he smiled, she couldn't help but waver.

She decided not to let her conversation with Phil dampen her spirits. After all, Christmas was next week, and then it wouldn't come again for another year. For eleven months, she alone would still have Christmas on her mind while the rest of the town started thinking about other holidays, and other seasons.

And Winter Carnival had a way of bringing out the best in people. Even in the Scrooges.

She'd sent Natalie off hours ago—it was the least she could do to make up for her absence from the booth yesterday. Sure, the ornaments were breakable, but technically she could manage. She was used to shuffling home from the grocery store with up to four bags in her hands at once, and the ornaments were considerably lighter. Still, she wouldn't refuse the gesture. Or the opportunity to spend a little more time with Phil.

"Thanks," she said, not quite matching his smile as he effortlessly lifted the remaining bags, saving her one trip back to fetch the last of her things.

"I didn't like how we left things off yesterday," Phil said, and this time, Cora felt the tension in her shoulders relax.

"I didn't mean to push you. Your family life is none of my business. I'm sure you'll make the choice that's best for you and Georgie."

"This parenting thing isn't easy," he said, raising his eyebrows.

"I wouldn't know, but I know how it feels to have a single father, and I can tell you that I'm very close with mine. I'm sure you and Georgie will be the same someday."

"What made things so close with you and your dad?" Phil asked.

Cora thought about it for a moment, then shrugged. "I guess it was the day-to-day things that I didn't even stop to appreciate half the time, but I just knew that I could count on him all the same. We never went on any big vacations, but he was there when I came home from school crying over a bad test grade, or when I didn't get the part in the tenth-grade musical, and I guess, just knowing that he was there and that he had my back, well, that's just about all I needed."

Phil shook his head. "Sounds nice. Can't say I ever had that experience with my father."

Cora squinted her eyes, wondering if she should ask about his falling out with the Keatons or let Phil open up when he was ready.

"My father was a workaholic. Still is. Can't say I ever even thought to share something about my day with him. I was too busy trying to find a way to impress him."

"But your grandparents are different," Cora pointed out.

Phil nodded. "My father wanted a different life than something he could have here, but I loved my trips. The family meals, the conversations. It was like a different world."

"And has it changed since you've been back?"

Phil hesitated. "It's exactly as I remembered." He sucked in a breath and looked behind him, where Georgie was trudging behind them in the snow, leaving marks in her track and yawning. "I think that Georgie ate her weight in your sisters' food this weekend. The mac and cheese was a big hit."

And warm, too. Amelia made several big vats of it every year, along with her famous chili and cornbread, and kept it warm on burners.

"Reminds me of when I was little," Cora said as they made their way onto the sidewalk. "Every year after the carnival, my parents used to round out the event by taking us on a sleigh ride through the orchard. The neighboring farm has horses," she explained.

"That sounds really special." Phil held out an arm to stop her from walking as a car abruptly pulled out of a spot.

She couldn't deny the pleasure she felt at such a simple gesture.

"It was special," she said as they continued toward the shop. Cora hadn't really thought of that in years. It was one tradition that they'd let slide, and she wasn't sure why. Maybe it was because she could only do so much to keep her sisters and her father from moping during the holidays. Amelia tried her best, cooking a feast just like their mother would have wanted, and she and Amelia both encouraged Maddie to make Christmas cookies, but Cora knew that if she hadn't insisted on the decorations, both indoors and out, and on the stockings, and the tree topper, and the hot chocolate and fire and classic holiday film on Christmas Eve, that all of those traditions would have slipped away, too.

Just like they were starting to do.

She righted herself as they crossed the street, not sure if she was being bold or just plain crazy, and said, "Maybe we could do that. For Georgie," she added quickly.

Phil grinned, but there was a spark in his eyes that she registered as hope. "Tonight?"

Cora shrugged. "Unless you have other plans."

"There's nothing more I'd like to do."

Cora felt as warm as if she were curled up with her favorite chenille blanket in front of the fireplace right now.

"Me either."

*

It didn't take long to set the bags of ornaments inside the store and make a quick call to her father, who then called Mr. Healy (also in his poker group), who was delighted to put the old sleigh to use.

"I nearly forgot that we used to do that," Cora told her father.

He was quiet for a moment. "I didn't."

Cora felt the tears begin to threaten, prickling the backs of her eyes. She swallowed hard and said thickly, "Thanks, Dad. I love you."

She hung up the phone feeling better than she had in weeks, and not just because she had the promise of a sleigh ride with Phil and Georgie to look forward to. A lot had changed in her family over the years, and certainly recently, but the old times, the ones she tried to protect and keep alive, were still with them.

They piled into Phil's car and Cora directed him to the farm, seeing that old Mr. Healy was already waiting for them inside the warm barn. The horses were magnificent, with rich chestnut brown coats that contrasted against the white snow, and a heavy plaid blanket was ready for them in the back of the sleigh.

"You get many rides this weekend?" Cora asked Mr. Healy as she settled onto the red velvet seat.

"No, this weekend most people are busy with the carnival. When you were little, your family used to make a point of stopping by afterward—I had the blankets washed and ready. Four little girls, always so delighted by the ponies, but especially you. Brings back good memories to see you here tonight, Cora." There was a twinkle in his eye as he grabbed the reins, and just like that, they were off.

"We're dashing through the snow!" Georgie cried out. "Just like in the song!"

Phil, who was seated in the middle, so Georgie could have an unobstructed view of the scenery, shifted a little closer to Cora. "This was a wonderful idea. Thank you."

It was a wonderful idea, but Cora was beginning to feel like she should be thanking him as much as he was thanking her. He'd inspired her to resurrect an old tradition, reminding her that there were other traditions than the ones she'd been clinging to—the ones her family was forgoing this year. So the angel wasn't on the top of their family tree. It was now on hers. And so Christmas Eve was abandoned. She had this.

She still had her traditions. Just not per se with her own family.

The trail led them all through the farm until the orchard next door was visible. Cora perked up in her seat and pointed, "See that big red barn over there? That's my family's orchard."

"I do recognize it," Phil said, leaning forward for a better look through the dark. "I remember my grandmother taking me when I visited in the summer. There was a shop in there, right?"

"The Sunday market." Cora nodded. "It closes for the winter months, but every Sunday we all had to help out, selling my mother's pies and jams, and of course whatever fruit was in season. My sister Maddie still makes pies each week, to carry on the tradition."

"There you go again with traditions," he said. "Makes me wish I had a few of my own."

An almost untraceable note of sadness crept into his tone, and Cora couldn't resist the opportunity to circle back to their conversation yesterday.

"What about with your grandparents? They had plenty. Didn't they pass down a few to your father?"

Phil shook his head. "My father wasn't interested in that sort of thing. He always felt restless here."

"And you?"

He waited a beat. "I loved it here. Just hating going back. But each trip to Blue Harbor was like a vacation, a fantasy world. Eventually, it was easier to just accept real life than to wish for a different one."

"This is real life to a lot of people," Cora told him. "Myself included."

Phil didn't look convinced. He didn't argue with her either.

"It's not too late, Phil. I mean, look at Georgie. These are memories she will always hold onto, you know?"

They turned to look at Georgie, who was now drowsy with sleep, a smile still resting on her face as evidence of a day well spent a night. The snow continued to fall softly all around them, glistening in the moonlight, and they fell silent taking it all in until they were once again parked in front of the old barn.

Phil stepped down first, then extended a hand to Cora. By now, Georgie was snoring softly, bundled up in the blankets for warmth.

Mr. Healy excused himself to get something from the main house, leaving them alone. Face to face. With the snow coming down around them, dusting Phil's dark hair.

Cora looked up into Phil's eyes, knowing that this was her cue. She should really thank him for the night, help rouse Georgie, and go back to her empty apartment for a mug of something warm. Only the way he was looking at her made her think that he didn't want that any more than she did.

He leaned in, and her heart began to thump. In the hushed night, she was nearly certain he could hear it. She closed her eyes as his mouth met hers, warm, slow, and soft. A perfect kiss for a perfect night.

They were interrupted by the sudden rustle of one of the horses, and Cora pulled back, seeing the desire in Phil's eyes and smiling to cover up her own feelings as Mr. Healy returned from the barn, holding a basket of cookies.

"Still warm from the oven," he said, handing them over to her. "My wife would have come out herself but she's on the phone with her sister in Chicago. Those two could talk for hours."

Cora laughed. "I understand completely. Thank you."

The moment was lost. Phil stirred Georgie from her sleep and together they all walked back to the car. It was late, it was time for Phil to get Georgie back to bed, and Cora knew that she'd have an early start at the shop.

They drove back into town in silence, listening to the carols playing on the radio. Cora handed Phil the basket of cookies. "Georgie will enjoy these more than me," she said.

He didn't argue with her there. "It's nearly Christmas."

She sighed. "Yes. It is." Normally this thought would thrill her, lift her with the same sense of joy and anticipation it always had since she was a child, but this year, it felt different, for a lot of reasons.

"I had a nice time tonight," Phil said, his voice low, as Georgie was slowly starting to drift back to sleep in the backseat. "I've, uh, had a nice time these past few weeks, actually."

"This town has a way of growing on people," Cora said with a little smile.

"I'm beginning to see that," Phil said.

Cora did her best to hide how much this pleased her. The more time he spent here, the less he'd want to go abroad, surely? And not just because of Georgie, but maybe, because of her, too.

Cora gave him one last smile and pushed the door open. Downtown Blue Harbor was quiet, the storefronts dark, making the lights and decorations all the more prominent.

Most people were either tucked into their warm beds or still at the town square, huddled around the bonfire, soaking in what remained of the season.

She knew that her family would still be there and that she could and maybe should carry on the newer tradition they had formed in recent years of joining them. But tonight, she didn't want to. She wanted to be alone, to think about what had transpired these past few days with Phil.

To think about the new traditions she'd started, and the ones that she still hoped to have. That was—if she could convince Phil that his daughter wanted him to stay.

That she wanted him to stay.

She went through the front door, seeing as it was late and the store was closed, and looked up at the mistletoe ball hanging over her head. She'd had her Christmas kiss tonight, and she had newfound hope too. Not just for this being the best Christmas ever, or for new traditions, but for something she hadn't even planned on: love.

13

Cora tended to divide her loyalty between the Firefly Café and Buttercream Bakery, even if Amelia had told her to give Maddie a boost during her opening weeks. Still, on Tuesday morning, Cora decided to stop by the café for a much-needed cup of coffee and a breakfast sandwich—something that Amelia had perfected over the years with the best blend of sharp cheddar cheese, roasted seasonal vegetables, and perfectly scrambled eggs. Not the typical holiday fare, maybe, but with Christmas Eve already being tomorrow, she didn't want to tire too quickly of all the spices and flavors of the holiday.

She nearly laughed at herself. As if she would ever grow old of all the pleasures of Christmas!

Still, an egg sandwich was what she craved, and maybe a little sisterly bonding too. Sure, Candy would be there, but she was becoming a fixture in their lives, and not just on the home front. Besides, she likely did send the tree to Cora and didn't even look for credit, making it sort of impossible to stay annoyed for too long.

It was the last big shopping day before Christmas, and even though most people in town had already purchased their decorations, there was always a big uptick in sales. People with out-of-town guests would be in need of some holiday-themed sheets or towels, and of course, last-minute gifts were always in demand. Cora was all too happy to guide her customers. A holiday apron for a sister who liked to bake? She was an expert by now.

In years past, she always closed the shop for the twenty-fourth, but now, with her sisters bailing on Christmas Eve, she wondered if she should rethink that. She supposed she'd see how the day went, and not just with sales.

Phil was still in town, and she didn't like to think that the days were closing in, but that rather, the chances of him staying a bit longer, or at least returning frequently, were growing by the hour.

She hadn't seen him since their kiss, and with her hectic schedule, she wasn't so sure she'd be able to break away either, no matter what Natalie said.

Was Phil really going to leave the day after Christmas after fulfilling his promise to Georgie—a day that was sure to guarantee even more sales, when she marked down the items that she didn't plan to resell next year, and everyone stopped in for a good discount? It was both an exciting day and a disappointing one, too. Decorating for Valentine's Day just didn't hold quite the same appeal....

Although, when she thought of that moonlit kiss, she had to consider that maybe this year she'd have more to celebrate than just a good excuse to eat too much chocolate.

Amelia was at the counter when Cora arrived, happy for the warmth and the smell of fresh coffee.

"You look happy today," her sister said as she approached.

Cora gave a little shrug. "It's Christmas week."

Amelia arched an eyebrow and reached for a to-go cup. She didn't need to ask Cora her order. "Is that all? Here I thought it might have something to do with you spending time with the Keatons' grandson. We all saw you two canoodling at the carnival, you know."

"Canoodling?" Cora lifted an eyebrow.

"I know! I know!" Amelia could only shake her head. "I've been spending way too much time with Candy."

Cora glanced to the left and then the right, careful that they wouldn't be overheard by the woman who had an ear for anything involving romance or gossip. She leaned across the counter and whispered, "He kissed me."

Amelia's eyes went so huge with surprise that Cora was almost afraid she might spill the coffee pot she was holding. Instead, she smiled broadly and said, "About time, Cora!"

"There you again. You sound as bad as Candy!" Cora teased, but she was pleased, and Amelia was right. It was about time. She'd just almost given up thinking that her time would ever come. She'd accepted her life for what it was. She had her shop. And it had been enough.

Until now.

"What can I say? I spend more time with Candy than my boyfriend." Amelia gave a weary shake of the head and they shared a laugh. "Speaking of which, I should go make sure she isn't burning that quiche. I'll be right back with your egg sandwich."

"You know me too well," Cora remarked.

"And for that reason, I won't be telling Candy that you and Phil are an item. Yet." Amelia winked and then disappeared through the swing door.

"Cora!" Cora turned to see Lanie Thompson coming toward her, smiling broadly. They'd always gotten along well.

"Lanie! Merry Christmas!"

Lanie extended a large breath and set a leather-gloved hand to her chest. "I'm happy to see you in such good spirits, Cora."

Cora blinked at her. She assumed by now that it was common knowledge in Blue Harbor that Christmas was her absolute favorite time of the year. "Of course!" She looked at Lanie quizzically. "I do run a holiday shop, after all." She laughed.

"So you're staying open? Good." Lanie fished into her pocket and retrieved a card that she thrust in her direction. "You know that I can help you find another space, just call me. Anytime."

Cora blinked down at the creamy white slip of cardstock that was being handed to her, unable to take it, much less understand what Lanie was saying.

"Another space?" she asked. "I'm pretty happy where I am."

Lanie winced. "I know, and I thought about that, too. Why not just rent from the new owner? Or buy it yourself, if you have the funds, right? But with the interest I've already received with investors looking to open an inn…"

Cora's heart was beginning to pound and she wasn't finding any of this funny anymore. She'd lost her polite smile somewhere through Lanie's speech and now she held up her hands, stopping her.

"Wait. An inn? Where my shop is? Where…my *home* is?"

Now it was Lanie's turn to pale. "You didn't know? Oh, Cora, I assumed you knew. That's why Phil Keaton came to town. He's handling his grandparents' estate. He's unloading their properties and cutting ties with this town."

Cora could feel the blood rushing in her ears, drowning out everything Lanie was still saying, now with clear concern in her eyes and a hand on Cora's wrist.

"I thought you knew. You and Phil have been spending so much time together and all…"

Of course that hadn't gone unnoticed. By anyone, it would seem.

Cora shook her head, feeling like a fool. "No. I had no idea. I thought…I guess I thought…"

She'd thought that he was spending time with her because despite all glaring evidence to the contrary, that he might just be falling in love with Blue Harbor.

And maybe, with her.

Only now, it made sense, didn't it? He never came back here. Blue Harbor wasn't his home. The man didn't even like Christmas. He was giving it one last go for Georgie's sake before he closed the door on his past for good.

Only she wasn't ready to say the same. Not without a fight. That store represented everything that was good about her life. Her fondest memories. The fact that hope and happiness could still shine through, lighting up even the darkest of times.

"We'll find you another storefront, honey," Lanie was saying, still thrusting the card at her.

Cora took the card and held it in her hands, even though she had no intention of using it. She didn't want another storefront. It wouldn't be the same. There would be no winding rooms for customers to meander through, and no themed spaces, either. There would be no tree lot next door come Thanksgiving. And there would probably be no upstairs apartment for her to live in, either.

Lanie's phone buzzed; she checked it with a dramatic roll of her eyes. "I completely forgot this appointment. I'd better run. But, you'll be okay, Cora," she insisted. She smiled her beatific smile, and for a moment, Cora almost dared to believe her. She squeezed Cora's hand before slipping away. "Call me. We'll find you something else!"

Only Cora didn't want something else. That shop was her second chance. Her fresh start. And her happy ending.

At least, that's what she'd thought…until Phil Keaton came to town.

She turned, leaving the café, forgetting her egg sandwich and knowing that if Amelia were to see her face right now that she'd instantly know that something was wrong. Very wrong. And that she'd want an explanation.

Only Cora couldn't give an explanation, because she didn't even have one for herself.

If Phil wanted to make her vacate, he'd had ample time to tell her, yet he hadn't.

This called for a visit. And not a cheerful one.

*

Cora knew she should go to the shop—with the activity she expected today, it seemed impossible not to be there bright and early. But it felt more impossible to think that come next week, she might not have a store at all.

Almost as impossible as the thought that Phil Keaton would be the one to take it away from her.

She hurried off a quick text to Natalie that she had important business to tend to and would be in as soon as possible, and hopped in her car, wasting no time in following the curving roads to the Keaton cottage.

In the morning light it looked small and sweet, the front path had been cleared of snow and there was the evidence of a Christmas tree in the front window. But the candles that Mrs. Keaton used to put at the base of each window ledge were gone, along with the wreath that always hung from their front door. Back when they'd lived in town, Cora had personally delivered each month's rent check. She knew that Mrs. Keaton loved to have company for a cup of tea and some conversation.

Today's visit wouldn't be so cozy. Or personal. This was strictly business.

If Phil was surprised to see her standing outside his front door, he did a good job of showing it. But then,

Cora thought with dismay, he was turning out to be quite the actor, wasn't he?

Still, her heart flip-flopped at the sight of that slow grin and the way his eyes crinkled at the corner as he held the door wider.

"Please tell me you're not here to carol," he said.

She wavered for a moment. Only a few days ago—heck, a few hours ago—she might have had a witty response to that, but today she was in no mood.

She shook her head. She was shaking, but not from the cold.

"Good. Georgie has had holiday music blasting all morning. Come in. You must be freezing."

More like boiling in rage, she thought. Still, she managed a tight smile and walked inside the house. It was warm, stifling really, but she didn't want to unravel her scarf or unbutton her coat or even shed her gloves. She wasn't here to make herself at home. She was here for answers.

In the distance, she could hear the music, and she hoped that Phil wouldn't ask Georgie to turn it down. This conversation was better kept between the two of them. If things went as she feared, it might not even turn out to be child-friendly.

"I can't stay long," she explained when he reached for her coat.

"Of course. The shop must be busy," he said, and she narrowed her eyes.

Like he cared. Or like it mattered, not if the store would be closed after the holidays.

She blinked back the tears that stung her eyes, threatening to fall, and held out the box, her excuse for coming, even though she had planned to give it to him this week anyway. Tonight, even. "I found this, in the shop," she explained as he popped the lid.

From the back room, the music was replaced with the sounds of a television. The soundtrack was unmistakable and one of her favorites. Under normal circumstances, she would have commented, eagerly asked to see Georgie, maybe even stayed to watch the holiday movie. But today she hoped that Georgie was too distracted by the film to pop her head out or say hello. Seeing her now, with those bright eyes and sweet smile, would make all of this much more difficult than it already was. And Cora couldn't lose her nerve.

She couldn't deny what she had been told. Even if that was all she suddenly wanted to do.

A day ago, this felt like the most hopeful Christmas yet. And now, well now she was starting to understand why some people didn't find it in their hearts to celebrate every year.

"Your grandmother collected them," Cora explained when Phil held up the small porcelain object in the shape of a dove. A peace offering, she realized, only she wasn't sure an ornament could make a difference now.

Not with someone who didn't understand the meaning of Christmas.

"I remember these…" Phil marveled.

"Well, you said that you didn't have any of the decorations, so when I saw this…I thought it might help you remember that one Christmas you spent here."

"You certainly like to uphold traditions," he said, the corner of his mouth lifting into a smile.

"If you don't carry on traditions, they slip away," she said, giving him a long look. It was what had happened to him, she realized now, to the Keatons, and everything they held so dearly.

And she'd vowed long ago not to let it happen to her.

"Have you decided what you plan to do with the house?" she asked, seizing the moment. "After the holiday?"

He raised his eyebrows, carefully returning the ornament to the box and avoiding eye contact. "Georgie is already asking about spending the summer here. She wants to swim in the lake."

Cora pursed her lips. "I'm not surprised."

He was finally forced to look at her, and when the smile fell from his mouth and his eyes shadowed, the silence confirmed everything she'd feared.

He blew out a breath. "To be honest, Cora, I had planned to sell the place. My grandparents don't need it. They won't be coming back. And…there didn't seem to be any point in holding on to it."

"And my shop? The property on Main Street?" She stared at him, half in challenge, half willing it to not be true.

He held her gaze for a beat before shaking his head. "I had no ties to this town, Cora. It's not personal."

"It is personal," she said in an angry whisper, not trusting her emotions to get the better of her when Georgie was in the next room. "It's very personal. That building isn't just my business. It's my home. And that shop…" She pulled in a shaky breath. He knew what that shop meant to her. To this town.

"I wanted to tell you, Cora, so many times. And then…"

"Yes," she said, straightening her back. "And then…what exactly? Tell me, Phil, because I'd like to know. What exactly was all of this? A way to soften the blow?"

"No!" he said. He pulled in a breath, raked a hand through his hair. "I came in that day when you were on the ladder. I had planned to tell you then."

She barked out a laugh. "Thanksgiving Day, you mean? You had planned to tell me on Thanksgiving that you were selling the property out from under me?"

She realized by the shame in his eyes that he hadn't even considered how poor his timing would have been. "I did. Yes." He shook his head. "I honestly didn't even think. The holidays never meant much to me."

"So I've noticed." It was cruel, perhaps, and by the hurt in his eyes, accurate.

"And then I came back the next day, hoping to tell you…and you were so good with Georgie. It was like overnight she changed. She was happy. I loved seeing her that way."

"Please," Cora said scornfully. "Don't pity me because I was nice to your child."

"I don't pity you," he said firmly. He was staring at her so intensely that she was momentarily disarmed. "I…I guess I'm in awe of you. I saw something in you that made me dare to believe that everything could be different. Better."

Tears welled up in her eyes and for a moment, she thought, it wasn't an act. It was all real. He was a good man. A man who loved his daughter. And this town. And Christmas.

And maybe even her.

But all too soon a shadow fell over his face again, and the warm and hopeful feeling was lost.

"This time here, this holiday…it's not our life. Georgie will be living with her mother again, and I have my business to think about, and everything I've worked for to get to this point. This has been a vacation, but you can't stay on vacation forever. Eventually, you have to go back to reality."

"You don't have to go back to the way things were," Cora said firmly, hating the emotion that threatened when her breath hitched. "And sure, a lot of people just come here for the summers, but a lot of people live here year-round, too. It's not a vacation for me. It's my home. My life."

And please don't take it all away, she thought.

He looked at her sadly for what felt like an eternity. She could hear the ticking of the old grandfather clock in the hall. Tears prickled the backs of her eyes, but they didn't fall. There was still hope. And Christmas was always a time for hope.

"You told me yourself that Blue Harbor was different—better—than the life you had back in the city," she said, hating the way her voice hitched. "And it doesn't have to be that way. Will you really be happier going back, putting your business before everything else, just to try to win your father's approval? Because I can tell you that you already have approval, just for being you. Your grandparents adore you as much as they love this town. And Georgie..." She trailed off. She'd said enough.

Phil's jaw tensed, and for a moment, she thought she had actually gotten through to him. Until he said, "I'm sorry, Cora. You know that I mean that."

"No," she said, taking a step backward, toward the door. She couldn't look at him, couldn't hear anymore. "I don't know that. And I don't believe it either."

She opened the door, letting the icy cold breeze hit her warm skin and freeze the tears that were hot and burning and about to spill over.

She stepped outside, knowing that this was probably the last time she would speak to him again, on a personal level, at least. There was still the business end of things to look forward to now, or maybe he'd spare her and have Lanie deliver the paperwork.

She turned, not giving any thought to what she was about to say, but allowing herself to speak from the heart, because when all else failed, that was what her mother had always told her to do.

"If you were sorry, you wouldn't do it. If you have to apologize, then you must know it isn't right. We all make choices, Phil. And saying you're sorry doesn't mean anything. Your actions do. And all the good intentions in the world don't help anything or anyone if your effort is put in the wrong place."

He stood tall in the doorway, the warm glow of the lamp in the hallway behind him. He stared at her sadly, not saying anything, until she turned and walked away, the snow crunching under her boots, all the way to where her car was parked. And even though she usually loved walking through the streets in this weather, days before Christmas when the wreaths were hung, and candles were lit in windows, and lights from Christmas could be seen in the corners of every house, each step felt heavier than the one before, because she wasn't walking toward anything anymore.

She was walking away from something. And someone.

And for the first time in a long time, all hope felt lost.

14

Christmas Eve this year was not like any Cora had spent before, and that wasn't just because Candy had spiked the hot cocoa with schnapps. She sat in the front room of her childhood home, with the fire crackling in the hearth and the Christmas tree lighting up the window, determined not to be bothered by the star that sat on top and finding that she had succeeded. Christmas was officially ruined; what did the tree topper matter?

Cora curled up tighter in her usual spot on the sofa, with the best view of the tree, of course, her favorite chenille blanket covering her legs, and a holiday movie playing on the television screen. By all standards, it was the same as always, except everything was different, and everyone was missing.

Cora didn't even protest when Candy suggested they watch a holiday movie of her choosing—a comedy that didn't give her any of the cozy vibes she'd cherished so much. Cora found that she rather liked the modern, colorized film to the usual black and white that she had memorized by now. Besides, she wasn't paying much attention to it anyway.

Her mind kept drifting back to the shop. And Phil. And every time she thought of the future and how uncertain it all felt, her stomach clenched, and she had to resist the urge to turn and talk to one of her sisters.

But they were not here. And that was why this Christmas Eve was not like any she had spent before. The movie and tree were just things. But the people…the people were what made Christmas so wonderful.

If only Phil could have understood that, Cora thought with a heavy sigh.

"How about I make us some more popcorn?" Cora's father broke the silence, and Candy was clearly relieved. Since walking in the door, unable to mask her feelings, Cora had told Candy and her father about her exchange with Phil, and Candy had made it her mission to cheer her up, saying they would together find an even better space, something fresh, something better.

Her smile never wavered, and not long ago this may have worn on Cora's nerves. But tonight she didn't mind the optimism, because she was fresh out of it herself.

Cora's father didn't wait for an answer as he collected the empty popcorn bowl that Candy had made short work of and moved slowly to the door, his old injury still flaring up from time to time.

"Extra butter and salt, Denny!" Candy grinned broadly as she turned to Cora. "If you're going to have a family movie night, you may as well double down."

Double down. That's what Cora had done, wasn't it? Put everything into her shop. Her money, her inheritance from her mother, her time. And, up until recently, her heart.

She'd given her heart to someone else. Let herself lose sight of what was most important. And now, she stood to lose it.

Catching her frown, Candy paused the movie and jostled next to her on the sofa. "Now, it's Christmas Eve. You're not going to tell me that you're going to let that man ruin this night for you? I know it's your favorite night of the year."

Cora gave Candy a weak smile. Her attempts at making the most of this holiday were obvious, from the light-up necklace she wore that was honestly making Cora a little dizzy, to the oversized elf slippers that left Cora wondering where she shopped, because none of these items were sold in her shop, to the endless supply of spiked cocoa, even if it was so strong that Cora was still only halfway through her first mug. Still, she was grateful for the refills of marshmallows every ten minutes or so. Candy was never one to do something halfway.

And neither, Cora supposed, was she.

"I don't know what I'm going to do, Candy," she admitted with a sigh. Tears prickled the back of her eyes and she blinked them away quickly. Took a sip from her drink instead. "That store was my entire life."

Candy nodded sagely. "It was. It's a terrible loss. But it's also, if you don't mind me saying this, maybe a blessing in disguise?"

Cora gaped at her. "How can this possibly be a good thing?"

Candy held up her hands defensively. "Now, just hear me out. Here you are, pretty as a Christmas card, sitting here with me and your father on Christmas Eve? Honey, that store is a wonderful place for you, and I know that your father couldn't be more proud, but maybe…well, maybe it's also been a good excuse for you to stay inside, tucked away, all alone. Maybe, if I may be so bold…" She paused. Candy was never anything if not bold. "Maybe you were a bit stuck in the past."

Cora fell quiet. She took a bigger sip of cocoa from her mug. The schnapps burned her throat, but it did the trick. She'd need to finish the rest if she was going to get through this conversation with Candy because Candy wasn't just being pushy for once.

She was also right.

"I suppose it was my safe place," she admitted. "Christmas had a way of boosting my spirits. Making me shut out all the tough stuff in life."

"And there's nothing wrong with a little joy and celebration. But I'm just saying," Candy continued. "It would do you good to get out more! Love doesn't just walk through the door."

Only in Cora's case, it sort of had. Or at least, so she'd thought.

Now she leaned her head back against the pillows, remembering the first time she'd seen Phil, when he'd pushed through the door of her shop, catching her by complete surprise. So much had changed since then, and not just the status of her business.

She'd changed, she realized. She now knew what it felt like to be with a man that she cared about, and to hold Georgie's hand in hers, to feel like a part of a family. A family different than the one that had once inhabited this big Victorian home.

Now she understood how her sisters were ready to spend their holidays elsewhere. Why they felt fulfilled with these new arrangements. That there was more to life if she was willing to take a chance.

Only after Phil had let her down, she wasn't so sure that she was.

"Popcorn is ready!" her father cried out from the hall. "Extra butter just for my lady."

Candy simpered, but her eyes glowed with happiness that was so contagious, even Cora couldn't help but smile. Her father had found a way to open his heart again. To make changes, and adjust.

Maybe she could too.

The doorbell rang just as they were about to get the movie started.

"Carolers?" Cora checked her watch. Normally she'd look forward to this—her cousin Jenna organized it every Christmas Eve with members of the choir, going door to door, singing one carol at each home, and it was always a surprise to see what you heard each year.

But tonight, Cora struggled to find the enthusiasm to push the blanket off her legs. She wasn't so sure she could fake the delight in Candy's expression.

But as it turned out, she didn't have to. A cold burst of winter air filtered into the front room and there, over her shoulder, stood not one, but all three of her sisters.

"What?" She blinked in surprise, but couldn't deny the smile on her face. "What are you guys doing here?"

"Change of plans," Maddie said, unwinding her scarf. Amelia and Britt were already untying their boots, and their father was taking their coats.

Cora looked at Candy, who didn't look surprised in the slightest. Come to think of it, neither did Cora's father.

"I'll just go make sure that popcorn is buttered to my standard," Candy said with a wink as she pushed off the couch and disappeared with Denny into the kitchen.

Cora's sisters descended upon her.

"We heard about Phil," Britt said. She sat directly in front of Cora, on the base of the hearth, shaking her head. "You know it will be all right, Cora. We'll make sure of that."

"There are other places on Main Street, or near it. I went through something similar when I thought I'd have to give up my space for the café," Amelia pointed out.

Cora nodded. "I know. It's not just about the move. It's about…the betrayal, I guess."

"I can't get over the nerve of that man! And the Keatons! Did you try calling them?" Maddie asked.

Cora shook her head. "They've been good to me. If this was what they wanted, then who am I to convince them otherwise? Maybe they need the money. And if they're not coming back to town, really, why do they need to hold onto all their properties?"

"But they loved this town," Maddie said, looking as confused as Cora felt. After all, Mrs. Keaton had loved her holiday shop more than nearly anyone else in town.

"It's the reality of their circumstances," Cora said, trying in vain to convince herself it was this simple. "And now mine."

"Just the same, I could throttle Phil Keaton for leading you on like that! Playing nice, just to let you down?"

Cora blew out a breath, feeling miserable. "I suppose that's exactly what he did. Tried to let me down gently. So much for that."

She thought of that kiss, in the snow, with the moonlight casting shadows over his handsome face.

Nope. No reason to go there. It had meant nothing, even though it had certainly felt like something.

"Well, you can't throttle him now," Amelia said.

"He left, Cora," Britt said when Cora looked at them all for an explanation. "Robbie was down at the gas station this morning and saw him filling his tank. He headed out of town."

Cora let this sink in. "I suppose all hope is lost then." For her shop. For love.

And for sweet little Georgie to have a proper small-town Christmas.

"Hey," Amelia said, giving her a little jab. There was kindness in her eyes that made Cora blink back tears. "You were always the one who said that Christmas was the time for hope, no matter how bad the rest of the year had been."

"Without you, Cora, I'm not sure what Christmas would have been like after Mom was gone," Maddie said with a little smile.

Cora's father came back into the room and handed her a glass of cider, clearly picking up on the fact that the hot chocolate wasn't to her liking. "It's true, honey. You were the one who always found a way to make the best of things. To keep going. You'll get through this. You just have to believe."

"In Christmas magic and all that stuff?" Cora pursed her lips.

"Maybe it's the time to believe in…yourself." Her dad gave a little wink and slipped away, leaving the sisters alone again.

"Is that why you all came over?" Cora asked. "To cheer me up?"

Even though she'd hated the thought of her sisters abandoning their beloved tradition, she didn't want to be the reason they sacrificed their own special plans.

"Consider it payback," Maddie said. "You cheered us up every Christmas, and now it's our turn to do the same for you."

"You guys…" Now Cora did brush away a tear. "What would I do without you?"

"Luckily you don't have to think about that," Amelia said as she pulled some of the blanket onto her own lap. "And between us, I can't think of any way I'd rather spend this evening. It's Christmas Eve. It's tradition."

And some traditions were meant to last, no matter what.

*

The drive back to Chicago was long, but the roads were clear, and traffic was light. Most people were at home, Phil supposed, wrapping presents, or waiting for relatives to arrive. Phil had a flashback to the one and only Christmas he'd spent in Blue Harbor, when his grandmother had been sitting in the front window when the car had pulled up. Now he wondered how long she'd been sitting there, waiting.

And he wondered with a sinking heart when she had stopped.

But unlike him, she hadn't stopped celebrating Christmas. She'd turned her community into her family.

"You sure that you're not too disappointed about today?" he asked Georgie, who had put up a fair and expected protest when he'd told her they were leaving this morning.

"I understand, Dad," was all she said. "Besides, it will be nice to see Great-Grandma and Grandpa."

That it would. It was long overdue.

The assisted-living community was a series of buildings, with snow-covered landscaping that was lit in the most cheerful way possible, but it was a small cry from the decorations in Blue Harbor, and Phil knew that his grandmother would especially be missing it.

He tried to remember which condo was theirs as he studied the grounds, the reminder that he'd only been here the one time making his gut tighten with guilt.

Finally, he saw it. The unmistakable glow of a Christmas tree in the window containing all the ornaments he hadn't found in the house—all the ornaments that he hadn't even remembered until he saw them. He parked the car and helped Georgie out so she didn't slip, and studied the tree through the window as they approached the front door. Sure enough, there were all the porcelain ornaments that Cora had mentioned.

His hand tightened on the bag containing the dove. A peace offering. One that was long overdue.

"You want to ring the bell?" he asked Georgie, who wasted no time in doing just that.

They waited, shuffling their feet to keep warm until the door opened, and there was his grandmother, in a bright red sweater, her eyes wide with confusion.

"Phil? And Georgie!" she cried happily as Georgie flung her arms around her waist. "But…I don't understand."

"We didn't want you to be alone on Christmas," Phil said, stepping inside the small living room where his grandfather was sitting on his favorite recliner, slow to stand.

He looked around the room that was decorated with all of his grandmother's most treasured decorations, ones that he still remembered from that one perfect Christmas, to the movie playing on the big screen in the corner, and the tree, that contained no gifts under it.

Yet.

He handed her the bag that Cora had given him, knowing that he had made the right choice in coming here.

"We don't want you to be alone on Christmas ever again," he said, squeezing his grandmother's hand as her eyes filled with tears.

And the same went for him, he thought, taking his daughter's hand with the other.

15

Even before Cora flipped her Christmas quilt off her flannel reindeer-printed pajamas and slid her feet into her matching slippers, she knew that it was going to be a good Christmas. Maybe not the best, maybe not perfect, but it was going to be good, because a long time ago she'd resolved to always make this one day of the year good, despite any other heartache.

She put on her robe and wandered into her living room, looking up at the big tree that and she and Phil and Georgie had decorated together, only this time, she didn't let her thoughts drift back to that special evening, or the disappointment that she felt since then. She looked up at the angel tree topper, sitting on a tree in an apartment that would soon be vacant, rather than in the big water-front Victorian where it had always been, and she knew that change was inevitable, but that somehow, in the end, things did find a way of working out.

She had to believe that, not just to keep her spirits up, but because it was Christmas.

And Christmas was a time for hope.

From downstairs, she heard a knocking at the back door, and she checked the clock as she hurried on the stairs, wondering if she'd slept in and one of her cousins or sisters had already come to collect her. She and Gabby had decided to drive over to the house together, seeing as they lived so close.

But it was Bart at the door.

For a second, Cora thought of what Candy had said about love not just showing up at the door, and wondered…

But no. Bart was a friend. A fellow Christmas enthusiast, at least part of the year. And he was a part of this town she loved so much.

"Still in the Christmas robe, I see," he said by way of hello.

She grinned. "Hey, it's Christmas. If there's any day I should get a free pass, it's today."

"Fair enough," he said. "And on that note, I wondered if you had figured out who sent the tree to you yet?"

Cora froze, remembering one of her theories, and if it was true, if Bart had sent her the tree. If she'd had love and romance all wrong all this time. Given the way that Phil had betrayed her, maybe she had.

But looking at Bart, tall and rugged, in his parka, she didn't feel anything more than a friendship.

"I wanted to tell you that when I was packing up last night, I came across the printed invoices and I saw who sent you the tree," he continued. "No digging or investigation. It was right there, so I thought, if you wanted to know…"

She nodded. It was Christmas. The tree would come down soon. And besides, she'd like to properly thank whoever had cared enough about her to think she needed it.

Because she did.

And so did that angel tree topper.

"It was that guy who was in town with his daughter. I saw you talking to him at the tree lot one night. Phil Keaton."

Cora blinked at him. Her mouth felt dry as she tried to process what he was saying. "Phil Keaton sent me that tree?"

Her mind was spinning, trying to think of why he'd done it, what motive he might have had. Why he hadn't ever confessed to doing it.

And despite everything that had happened, and everything he'd done, she knew that he hadn't sent it to ease the blow. He'd sent it because he cared.

And that maybe she hadn't been so wrong about love after all. Maybe sometimes it just wasn't meant to last.

*

After Bart left, complete with his annual gift—a new ornament for his own tree back home, because what else do you give to a guy who sells trees for a living—Cora walked through her shop, stopping to admire her favorite displays, the treasured pieces she had collected over the years, hoping to share her love for the holiday with all those she loved most. Hoping that people would come into her store and buy something special, something that might become a tradition of their own someday.

Even if just for a little while.

Plans changed, and people adapted, and traditions did too, she knew now.

She stopped at the counter and picked up the snow globe her father had given to her on Thanksgiving, thinking of all the wishes that had been made on it, even if they had only partly come true. It was one special item from her mother, her mother who believed that Christmas was full of magic and possibility.

And an open heart.

Cora hadn't bought anything for Candy yet—she still hadn't thought of the right gift. But now, she wrapped the snow globe in tissue and tied the most festive bow she could around the box she set it in.

Candy had come into their lives and nothing had ever been the same since, and that was not a bad thing at all. It was, in many ways, a gift in itself.

She went upstairs to shower and dress, and then hurried back downstairs with all the carefully wrapped gifts, to find Gabby's flower delivery truck parked outside, Gabby inside waiting. Inside the warm vehicle, the radio was turned to the Christmas station—something her cousin had done just for her.

The roads were quiet and still, and Cora knew that everyone was tucked inside their homes, enjoying the holiday with their family.

Her own childhood home was far from quiet. The house was full when they arrived—of presents, and music, and laughter, and conversation. Aunt Miriam and Uncle Steve were already there, as were Jenna and Cora's sisters. And their significant others. Candy was wearing a beautiful off-white sweater dress, Cora noticed, stopping to pay her a compliment.

"I did it to go with your theme of White Christmas," Candy said. "I can't wait to see how you set up the table."

It wasn't a Christmas tree, but it was a peace offering, and before Cora could escape, Candy wiggled her fingers and pulled her in for one of her good, long, squishy hugs. And Cora could only laugh and wonder what her mother would think, and know in her heart of hearts, that she'd be smiling. From ear to ear.

After setting up the dining table, which was stretched to full capacity with two leaves, Cora entered the kitchen where Amelia and Maddie were hard at work on the center island, Maddie on a pie crust, and Amelia peeling potatoes. "You need any help?"

"Just prepping while I have time," Amelia said. "But if you want to help me, you can keep Candy out of the kitchen."

"It's practically her kitchen now," Cora pointed out, and the room fell silent. It wasn't long ago that this entire house was silent, but now, at this moment, it was full of Candy's singing—because she loved any chance to put those pipes to use—and her laughter, and their father's laughter too. And it was nice to know that even when they all went back to their own homes, to their lives, and maybe even to their traditions, that this house was still full of life.

"You okay with that?" she asked her sisters, who had spent more time in this room than she had.

They gave each other a glance and smiled. "Change isn't easy, but it's often worth it." Amelia gave her a meaningful look. "It will all work out, Cora, I believe that."

Cora pushed back the heaviness in her heart when she thought of her shop and the meandering rooms that she'd so carefully decorated. This weekend she'd look at some other spaces, figure out how to make one of them work, and hope that she could cover the lease, even if her father had offered to help bridge the gap if need be.

"I suppose I'll finally have to cut back on merchandise," she said to her sisters, but they didn't give her the knowing look she'd expected. If anything, they looked just as disappointed for her as she felt.

The doorbell rang, cutting through the din of the house, and Cora and her sisters exchanged questioning glances. They were all accounted for until Aunt Miriam's sister's family arrived for dessert, unless a neighbor had decided to stop by.

"I'll get it," she said, seeing that her sisters were otherwise occupied. She walked down the hall and opened the door and saw, to her surprise, Phil standing on the porch, shivering in his expensive wool coat.

"Phil." She stared at him, not sure what to say, or why he was here. More details of the eviction to work out? He didn't seem to honor holidays when it came to business, after all. "I thought…I heard you left town," she managed.

He gave her a little grin. Really, what was there to smile about? The man had thrown her to the curb, at Christmastime!

"I did leave, and I have you to thank for that."

She folded her arms across her chest, but not because she was cold. No, she was downright steaming mad. Showing up at her family home, on Christmas. He had better have something good to say.

She sucked in a breath. She didn't dare hope. Not even on Christmas. But Christmas was the time to hope, and oh, she wanted to believe that this wasn't going to just be a good Christmas, but the best one yet.

"How did you know where my family home was?" she asked him.

He grinned wider. "Like you said, everyone knows everyone in Blue Harbor. And my grandparents pointed it out."

"Your—" She blinked, then looked past him to the luxury SUV that was sitting out front, the engine still running. Through the tinted windows, she saw a shadow of Mrs. Keaton's face, and a hand waving at her. "Your grandparents are here?"

"That's why I left," Phil explained. "I was thinking about what you said, about how much my grandmother loved Christmas. And then I thought of her alone with just her husband."

He frowned and looked down at his shoes. Cora resisted the urge to set a hand on his arm. However touching this gesture might be, the man had still evicted her from not only her apartment but also her place of business.

"When I saw how much Georgie loved the town's traditions, I knew just how much my grandparents must miss them."

Cora nodded, forcing herself not to get too soft here. "Well, I'm sure they're thrilled to spend one last holiday in Blue Harbor."

"Oh, it won't be the last," Phil said, flashing a grin.

Her heart skipped a beat, and for a moment she almost didn't trust herself to speak. To hope.

"It wasn't just Georgie who loved being here for Christmas. It was me, too. Then, and now. I had one perfect Christmas in this town a long, long time ago. And again, more recently."

His gaze was steady. "You made me a believer, Cora. You made me realize what Christmas is all about, and what it really means, and I'm not so willing to walk away from it again." He looked her in the eye. "Or you."

Her voice was locked in her throat. "Phil…"

He held up a hand. "Please. There's something I need to say, Cora. I came to town with clear intentions. I buy out businesses. I close them down. I look at the numbers and I do what makes sense, practically, not emotionally. What I always thought was the right step. I never bother to get to the heart of the matter, to know the faces behind the door. But I got to know you. And the more I got to know you, the harder it became to go through with things."

She raised an eyebrow. "But you did. You told me in the end."

"I did. And once it was out, it confirmed everything that I've known since I came here." He took a step toward her, his smile replaced with a look far more serious. And maybe, more sincere. "You reminded me of all the good things I used to feel when I was in Blue Harbor. All the simple things that brought my child so much joy. That brought me joy. All this time, I've been chasing something that wasn't real. All I know is that I was empty before."

"So you're not going overseas?"

He shook his head. "No. No, I can't leave Georgie like that. Not now. Not when I see what I can have with her. What I found with her. And I can't leave my grandparents either. I'm all they've got. Well, me and this town."

"You mean they're moving back?" She thought of what he'd said about Mr. Keaton's health.

"But—"

He nodded. "But nothing. This is where they belong. And it's where I belong too."

Tears prickled the back of her eyes, and even though she told herself it was due to the wind, she knew it wasn't true.

"You showed me the meaning of Christmas," he said to her. He reached out to take her hand. His were cold in hers, but they warmed slowly. "You made me see the meaning in a lot of things."

"Blue Harbor has a way of doing that to people," she said humbly.

"Oh, I know," he said, grinning. "It got under my skin a long time ago, but you…you stuck."

Cora sensed a shuffling behind her and whispers as everyone frantically dispersed. Of course Candy lingered a little longer—her perfume was evidence of that. Cora was letting in a draft, but she wasn't ready to close the door just yet.

Or ever.

Candy had said that love didn't just show up the door, but it had for Cora. Twice. And things like that didn't happen without a little Christmas magic.

"We have room," she said, giving him a little smile. "If you all want to join us?"

"I can't think of anything better," he said, his grin widening. "Except one thing."

He stepped closer, until there was no more space left between them, and then he kissed her. Right under the mistletoe.

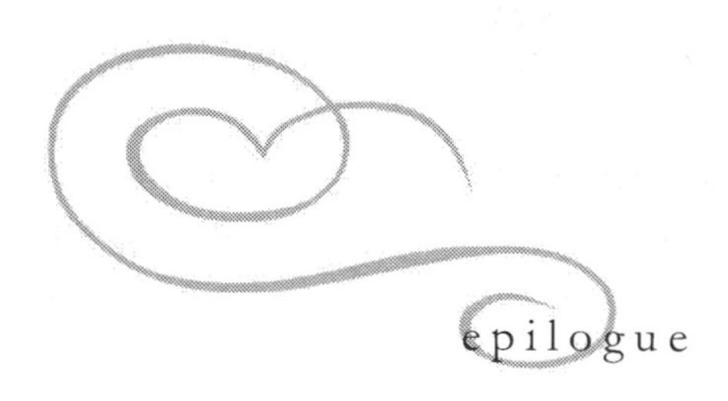

epilogue

The pub at the Carriage House Inn was crowded on New Year's Eve, just as it always was, not that Cora would know. Even when her sisters encouraged her to get out each year, Cora usually found an excuse to stay home in her flannel pajamas with a good book.

But this year, her sisters were all on dates with their significant others.

And so was Cora.

She grinned at Phil across the table, who had insisted that they celebrate their sledding win tonight, as a proper date.

"You're sure that Georgie won't feel bad that it's just the two of us?" Cora asked again, thinking that really, it had been a team win.

"She's back at the cottage with my grandparents," Phil said, brushing away her concern. It was Georgie's second to last night in town before she'd go back to live with her mother, but she'd be back again in two weeks. Now that Phil was planning to divide his time between Chicago and Blue Harbor until he sold his business, Georgie would come to town for her more frequent weekends with him.

"Have you decided what you're going to do, once you sell the business?" she asked, knowing that he was having fun with the thought of the sale, seeing that it was something he was an expert at, after all.

"Nope," he said, and then burst out laughing. "And isn't that wonderful?"

Cora grinned. It was wonderful, and for so many reasons. "You know, I should probably tell you that you changed the way I see Christmas too."

He looked at her skeptically. "Don't tell me I've turned you into a Scrooge."

She laughed. Like that could ever happen, though she had been tested. "You made me see that life moves forward. That we can't let ourselves get stuck in the past. That sometimes new traditions are actually better than old ones."

He gasped dramatically and then winked. "I can't take all the credit, though. Georgie told me you made a wish on that snow globe…"

Cora felt her cheeks flush. She might be the Christmas lady and a little Christmas crazy, too, but she was on a date, and she could just feel her sisters giving her warming glares, even though they were nowhere around.

"Well, now, it was just a snow globe…"

"Oh, not just any snow globe!"

Cora looked up to see her father and Candy standing beside their table. Candy was dressed in gold. And silver. And lots of sequins, because, well, it was New Year's Eve. And this was Candy.

And Cora rather loved her for it.

"As it turns out that wishing ball works," Candy said with a grin. She held out her left hand, where a sparkling diamond sat on her ring finger, catching the light that shone nearly as bright as the joy in her eyes.

Cora stared at the ring and then up to her father, seeing the same happiness reflected in his smile that she felt in her heart of hearts.

Yep, life kept moving forward, no matter how hard you tried to hold onto the past.

And Cora couldn't wish for anything more.

ABOUT THE AUTHOR

Olivia Miles is a *USA Today* bestselling author of feel-good women's fiction with a romantic twist. She has frequently been ranked as an Amazon Top 100 author, and her books have appeared on several bestseller lists, including Amazon charts, BookScan, and USA Today. Treasured by readers across the globe, Olivia's heartwarming stories have been translated into German, French, and Hungarian, with editions in Australia in the United Kingdom.

Olivia lives on the shore of Lake Michigan with her family.

Visit www.OliviaMilesBooks.com for more.

Made in the USA
Monee, IL
08 November 2021